WILD RESCUERS
ESCAPE TO THE MESA

And don't miss

Wild Rescuers: Guardians of the Taiga

WILD RESCUERS

ESCAPE TO THE MESA

Stacy Hinojosa aka *Stacy Plays*

ILLUSTRATED BY Vivienne To

HARPER
An Imprint of HarperCollinsPublishers

Photos on pages 187–192 courtesy of StacyPlays

Photos on pages 193–197 courtesy of Coyote Peterson

Wild Rescuers: Escape to the Mesa

Text copyright © 2019 by Stacy Plays LLC

Interior illustrations copyright © 2019 by Vivienne To

www.harpercollinschildrens.com

ISBN 978-0-06-279640-0 — ISBN 978-0-06-291500-9 (special ed)

Typography by Jessie Gang

19 20 21 22 23 PS/LSCH 10 9 8 7 6 5 4 3 2 1

❖

First Edition

For Page

CONTENTS

MAP . . . . x–xi

CAST OF CHARACTERS . . . . xii–xiii

CHAPTER ONE 1

CHAPTER TWO 12

CHAPTER THREE 23

CHAPTER FOUR 31

CHAPTER FIVE 38

CHAPTER SIX 48

CHAPTER SEVEN 57

CHAPTER EIGHT 68

CHAPTER NINE 73

CHAPTER TEN 83

CHAPTER ELEVEN 95

CHAPTER TWELVE 102

CHAPTER THIRTEEN 108

CHAPTER FOURTEEN 119

CHAPTER FIFTEEN 127

CHAPTER SIXTEEN 139

CHAPTER SEVENTEEN 147

CHAPTER EIGHTEEN 157

CHAPTER NINETEEN 167

CHAPTER TWENTY 174

STACY'S FAVORITE WORDS

FROM THE BOOK 181

THE REAL-LIFE MESA BIOME! . . 187

MEET THE REAL-LIFE MOLLY! . . 191

GET TO KNOW

AN ANIMAL EXPERT! 193

ACKNOWLEDGMENTS 201

WILD RESCUERS
ESCAPE TO THE MESA

ghost town

NORTH
to Taiga

pueblo town and station

Stacy

Everest

Wink

Basil

Tucker

Addison

Noah

Page

Milo

Molly

Quail

Jack Rabbit

Mountain
Lion

Droplet

Splat

Donkey

WILD RESCUERS
ESCAPE TO THE MESA

ONE

LICK.

Lick.

Lick.

A smile crept across Stacy's face as the small dog nuzzled her awake.

"Hi, Page," Stacy said groggily.

It was strangely cold in the cave. Stacy opened her eyes, instantly aware that she and Page were alone.

Typically, Stacy slept nestled among her pack of Arctic wolves, their soft white fur providing Stacy with more warmth than any blanket or comforter ever could. And usually, the wolves waited for Stacy to wake up. But this morning was different. Her wolves were gone.

Panic began to bubble up inside of her as she frantically rubbed her eyes and looked around until she spotted them. They weren't gone at all; they just weren't cuddled beside her. Everest, the alpha of the pack, was guarding the entrance to the cave. He was exchanging looks with Tucker, who was also at the cave entrance. Stacy remembered that last night had been Tucker's turn to do patrol duty on the ridge. He must have just returned to update Everest on the evening's events.

Basil, the beta of the pack, was curled up by the cave's hearth, where a healthy fire was crackling. *Silly Basil,* Stacy thought to herself. *She survives being struck by lightning and yet she still likes to start fires.* Addison, the pack's other female wolf, was sitting near the large spruce table in the cave where Stacy prepared the pack's meals and did various crafting projects. Behind her, Noah splashed in the small freshwater spring that flowed through the back of their cave. That was all her wolves accounted for—all except . . .

"Where's Wink?" Stacy asked, sitting up. *He shouldn't be out by himself.* The fire that had spread through the taiga a couple of months before had driven all the hunters away for a while, but Stacy suspected there might still be a bounty on the wolves. Which meant they could all be in danger.

Suddenly, Wink came bounding into the cave. At least, Stacy was pretty sure it was Wink. It was hard to tell because his normally brilliant white fur was brown, as if he'd been rolling in dirt. His front paws were completely covered in mud, which he was now tracking into the cave. Everest growled quietly in dismay at the mess. Wink sauntered up to Stacy and innocently dropped a mouthful of crumpled peonies on her lap.

Stacy blinked a couple of times and looked at the pink flowers. They were covered in slobber and were already beginning to wilt. It was almost like Wink had dug them up in the forest days ago and then buried them until this morning. Actually, that was exactly what it was like. But why?

What is going on? Stacy thought. *First my wolves are all up and about without me. Now these flowers?* And then it hit her. Today must be the eighth day of October. Today was her "rescue day."

Since no one knew when Stacy's birthday was, they'd celebrated her rescue day every year since she'd come to live with the wolves in the taiga forest. This was year number five. Every morning of her rescue day, each wolf would give Stacy a gift to mark the occasion. How the wolves kept track of which day it was, Stacy hadn't a clue. Nor was she sure of the exact details of the events that led to her being rescued and taken in by six Arctic wolves in the first place.

Any memories Stacy had of those events were buried deep in her mind. No matter how hard she tried, she couldn't remember anything. It wasn't like she could ask the wolves. Over the years, the group had developed their own way of communicating with each other through barks, facial expressions, and body language, but they couldn't talk or write—although Stacy was convinced that Addison was trying to learn how to read.

"Thank you, Wink," Stacy said, picking up the flowers and cradling them in her arms. "These were . . . uh, I mean, these *are* beautiful."

Wink stared up at her expectantly. "Oh, you're right, I didn't smell them," Stacy said as she brought the droopy blooms up to her nose. "Mmm. So sweet." She set the flowers down beside her. Page sniffed them and immediately buried her nose in her paws.

Stacy stood and walked across the cave to her rocking chair and took a seat. She knew what was coming next. One by one the other wolves were going to bring her a gift.

Sure enough, Tucker was already making his way toward her, dragging something behind him. Stacy leaned out of her rocking chair, craning her neck. As soon as she saw what it was, she let out a tiny gasp and stood up. Tucker was bringing her a large bow and a quiver filled with arrows. He pulled it as far as Stacy's feet and then looked up at her nervously, waiting to see if Stacy would be happy about being gifted a weapon on her rescue day.

"Wow," Stacy said reverently, crouching to the cave floor and running her fingers along the bow. "Tucker, how did you get this?"

Tucker's rust-colored eyes danced around the cave. It wasn't like Tucker to steal from people who came into the taiga. But if there was one thing Tucker hated, it was hunting. He must have swiped it from a hunter knowing Stacy would only use it for good. And with everything that happened over the summer with the wolf bounty, including the time when Dusky, the alpha of the wild wolf pack, was shot, Stacy was grateful to have another way to protect herself and the pack besides her small knife.

"Thank you, Tuck," Stacy said. "I'll have to practice a lot, but I'm glad you brought me this. For now, though, why don't you put it on my desk over there . . . out of Page's reach."

Tucker eagerly obliged, pulling the bow and quiver of

arrows onto the flat boulder Stacy used as a desk. Then Addison took a step toward Stacy and pointed her snout toward the crafting table, where a pumpkin pie, Stacy's favorite, was cooling. Addison had baked it by the fire in an old tin they'd found at a campsite. Stacy knew wolves weren't supposed to know mathematics, but Addison did (another reason why Stacy suspected she knew how to read). That knowledge made the graceful wolf particularly proficient in things like baking, where exact measurements were required.

"Addi, that smells delicious, thank you," Stacy said, sitting back down in her chair. Addison beamed with pride.

Next was Noah, who had walked over while Stacy had been examining the bow. He proudly presented Stacy with some wet clay he'd fished up from the river banks.

"Thanks, boy," Stacy said, turning the soft clay over in her hands. She looked at Wink. "We can use this to make a flowerpot. Then the next time you bring me peonies they won't die so quickly."

Wink wagged his tail and Stacy gave both him and Noah a pat on their heads.

Stacy got out of her chair and walked over to a sullen-looking Basil. The scar from where Basil had been struck by lightning during July's thunderstorm was almost healed. New fur was beginning to grow in where the worst burns had been. After the fire, Stacy and the wolves had spent the rest of the summer lying low in the cave and caring for Basil.

The lightning strike had seemed to affect Basil more on the inside than the outside. It had weakened her and she'd had to learn to walk all over again. She was able to walk short distances now, but was in no shape to leave the cave to find Stacy a present.

"The best gift you could *ever* give me is to get better, girl," Stacy said, kneeling down beside her and gently cupping Basil's muzzle in her hands. "I mean that."

Basil stared up at Stacy, her giant yellow eyes finding Stacy's emerald green ones. Stacy kissed Basil's head and turned to look at Everest, who had appeared next to her in front of the fire. His silver eyes bore a serious expression.

"Everest," Stacy started. "It's okay if you didn't get me anything either, I . . ."

Stacy's voice trailed off as she noticed Everest was holding something in his jaw. He lowered his head to where Stacy's hands were. She turned her palms up and he dropped the small item into them.

Stacy stared blankly at the object in her hands. It

felt . . . familiar. It was a small silver charm bracelet. Stacy squinted her eyes, hoping that the memory attached to the bracelet would somehow come into focus.

She examined the charms; they had a dirty gray patina to them. There was a horse, a book, a helicopter, a letter S, and a mermaid.

"Everest," Stacy whispered. "Where did you get this?"

She looked up at Everest, who had a sad, wistful expression on his face.

Stacy knew, of course, that he couldn't answer her. Still, she waited to see if Everest would make some gesture to give her a clue about where the bracelet came from. Instead, he walked past Stacy and lay down next to Basil. Stacy frowned for a moment. *Why is he acting so odd?*

"Thank you, everyone," Stacy said, turning to address the entire pack. "You've made this the best rescue day ever."

The wolves looked around at each other, obviously pleased with themselves.

Stacy retreated to the back of the cave to change out of her pajamas and into her everyday clothes—a pair of worn blue jeans and her favorite blue-and-white-striped long-sleeved T-shirt. The shirt was incredibly soft from years of wear. Sometimes Stacy had to stop herself from sleeping in it, too. She didn't want to wear it out too fast—she and Addison had already sewn patches onto both of the threadbare elbows, which had ripped open during their last animal rescue—a small pine marten who had injured its leg. Tucker had devised an ingenious splint for it using a discarded tent stake which he'd affixed onto the little mammal with some moss and tree sap that would likely break away after a few weeks of healing.

Stacy walked over to her little makeshift bookcase in the cave and set the charm bracelet down on one of the shelves. She couldn't quite put her finger on it, but something about Everest's body language made Stacy think he hadn't just found it in the woods. The bracelet felt so familiar. She was sure she had seen it before. *Why can't I remember where?*

She looked up at the top of the bookcase, where her pet chicken, Fluff, roosted. Stacy reached her hand under Fluff and pulled out a speckled egg. Digging her hand into her pants pocket, she pulled out a handful of seeds.

"Here's your breakfast, girl," Stacy said, patting her feathers. "Thank you for mine."

Stacy walked across the cave and set the egg down in front of Addison, who was tidying up as Wink and Page chased each other around the crafting table.

"I'm going to scramble that when I get back, okay?" Stacy said to Addison, walking over to the cave entrance and peering outside. It was drizzling, but she could see through the mist and clouds that the sun was just coming up over the giant spruce trees to the east.

"We're late," Stacy said to the pack, pulling on her leather boots. She tied the right one up while Everest, carefully holding the laces in his teeth, tied the left. Stacy stood and grabbed her old leather satchel that hung on a hook near the cave entrance. She turned around to see Everest and Basil waiting for her command.

"Okay, let's go," she said. "You too, Page. Droplet and Splat will be expecting us."

TWO

STACY, EVEREST, BASIL, and Page trudged through the muddy taiga on their way to visit Droplet and Splat. Everest, as usual, was about twenty paces ahead, always on the lookout for potential threats to his pack.

Stacy knew of two big threats that Everest was watching for: the first one being it was officially hunting season, so they had to avoid any hunters who might be tracking deer or moose. The second and more serious threat was the wolf bounty the village had imposed over the summer to control the wild wolf pack that had started killing sheep from a farm on the outskirts of the village for food. The bounty meant farmers could legally kill wolves, and, adding insult to injury, get paid for doing so. It made Stacy's blood boil.

She'd made her pack go into hiding for most of the summer because of it, and because of Basil's injury. But there was no trace of the wild wolf pack anymore. And the damage from the forest fire kept a lot of people from hiking or hunting near their cave, so she'd thought it was safe to resume their daily outings. Stacy always accompanied the wolves during the day, though. She figured that no farmer would shoot one of her wolves if a little girl was standing right next to it. Hopefully, they would assume she was just out walking her large dogs.

Basil gave a little impatient growl. Stacy could tell she was frustrated by how slow she needed to walk because of her injuries. Basil's job before the lightning strike had been that of the pack's scout. She was the fastest wolf in the pack and could easily run ahead of everyone, survey the forest, and then run back and tell the group which direction to go.

"You're getting stronger every day, girl," Stacy said quietly to Basil so Everest wouldn't hear. "I bet you'll be running circles around him again by Christmas." Basil seemed to stifle a laugh. *Do wolves laugh?* Stacy wasn't sure, but she was happy she'd been able to bolster Basil's spirits, if only for a moment.

Droplet and Splat, the timber wolf pups Stacy had rescued from the forest fire, were now living at Stacy's farm, a small clearing hidden deep in the taiga where Stacy and the wolves kept a little crop of pumpkins and root vegetables.

It was hard for Stacy to believe it had been almost three months since the wolf pups came to live with them. Stacy and Everest had searched for weeks for any remaining members of the wild pack who might have returned to their burned-down den after the forest fire. Even if the pups' mother had died in the fire, Stacy knew all the members of the pack would help rear cubs. But they'd found no trace of them.

Stacy guessed the survivors had moved on to a new territory. And she didn't blame them if that was the case—between the firefighting crews and the land surveyors taking measurements for the proposed ski and golf resort, not to mention all the usual hikers and campers, there had been a lot of human activity in the taiga over the summer. Wolves want nothing to do with humans. Stacy's pack was unique in the fact that they allowed Stacy to live with them.

The pups stayed with the pack in the cave for a few weeks after the fire, but had quickly outgrown the space. They'd needed more room to run around and practice the hunting skills Everest had been teaching them. It was a little strange to Stacy for Everest to be teaching Droplet and Splat how to hunt the small taiga animals Stacy and her pack spent their days rescuing, but she understood that it was part of the cycle of nature. She also knew that growing pups could not adapt to the unusual diet of fish, pumpkins, and berries that Stacy and the pack ate.

Besides needing more room to run, the wolf pups had also had a difficult time adhering to the group's sleep schedule. Wolves are most active at dusk and dawn (and sometimes in the middle of the night), but Stacy's wolves had adopted the particularly human habit she had of sleeping when it was dark. Now, whichever one of Stacy's wolves had patrol duty for the night also looked in on Droplet and Splat to make sure they stayed out of trouble.

Stacy had named Droplet and Splat one morning while she watched Noah trying to teach them to fish. Back then, Stacy had hoped the pups would develop a love of salmon instead of rabbit. But instead of watching Noah as he expertly caught fish after fish for them to eat, the pups kept playing in a small waterfall in the river. Droplet eagerly lapped up the water, sticking her whole head into the stream to drink and then shaking off, sending water droplets flying in all directions. Splat, on the other hand, sat directly in the small falls, happily letting the water beat down on his head, matting his fur down around his eyes.

Stacy had thought of the nicknames on the spot, never intending them to be their actual names, but they seemed to suit their personalities and so they stuck.

It was a good thing, Stacy thought, that the wolf pups

were staying more *wild* than her pack. They didn't have the special abilities her pack had—they couldn't understand Stacy when she spoke to them, other than a few basic commands. Their wildness also meant they would be free to leave the taiga if they wanted to when they were older. And if the construction company from the village got their way, and the taiga was transformed into a ski and golf resort, Droplet and Splat might not have any choice but to find a new home.

Sometimes Stacy wondered what her wolf pack would be doing if they weren't living with her and helping her to rescue animals around the forest. *How had six Arctic wolves come to live outside of the Arctic in the first place?*

Stacy pushed the question to the back of her brain as they reached the farm. The pine and spruce trees were incredibly dense in this part of the taiga. Stacy needed to hold both hands out in front of her face to push away the needle-filled branches all around her. Everest lowered his head to the forest floor and pulled away some branches to reveal the small underground passageway they used to enter the farm. Stacy, Basil, and Page followed him, shimmying their way through the passage and up into the clearing. There, nestled among the pumpkins and orange and yellow fallen leaves, were Droplet and Splat, fast asleep.

"Typical teenagers," Stacy scoffed. She felt a little silly for telling the others that Droplet and Splat would be waiting for them.

"Wake up, you two," Stacy said. "Everest is here for your lesson."

Droplet opened one of her eyes to peer groggily at

Stacy while the other stayed shut. Splat rolled onto his back and began snoring loudly.

"All right," Stacy said, reaching into her satchel. "I was going to save this for after your lesson, but it seems like you both need a little bit of motivation today."

She pulled a small newspaper-wrapped parcel out of her bag and unwrapped it, revealing a partially eaten rabbit carcass. At least, Stacy thought it was a rabbit. It was a bit hard to tell at this point. Immediately, Stacy spotted Splat's nose twitching. Droplet's other eye flashed open.

Within a couple of seconds, both juvenile wolves were sitting at attention at Stacy's feet. Page sat next to them, eyes wide, hoping to get a piece of the gruesome mid-morning snack. Stacy turned to Everest and Basil, whose jaws were hanging open with surprise.

"What?" Stacy said innocently. "A bald eagle dropped it in front of me while I was going to the bathroom this morning. What was I supposed to do?"

Taking extra care not to touch the rabbit, Stacy flung the paper away from her and tossed the carcass to Everest.

"Here, you take it," she said to the alpha wolf, motioning toward Droplet and Splat. "Maybe you can use it to do some kind of scent drill with them."

Everest caught the carcass in his mouth and took off, running out of the clearing with Droplet and Splat close on his heels. Page looked pleadingly at Stacy, who shook her head.

"Stay, Page," she said in a commanding tone. Page was fast, but there was no way she could keep up with the wolf pups when they ran, and Stacy didn't want her to get lost. "All right, Basil. Let's get to work, shall we?"

Basil nodded and began walking in a slow circle around the clearing. Stacy found the wooden hoe she'd carved out of a fallen birch branch last year and began to dig up a couple of potatoes. She would bake them for supper in the coals of Basil's fire back at the cave.

"Just let me know when you're ready, girl," she said to Basil. Stacy pulled her knife from the leather holder attached to one of her belt loops. She sliced off the end of one potato, cutting off a small nub known as an eye, and replanted it in the ground so a new potato would grow. She used the hoe to fill in the hole and patted the soft dirt until it was firm.

Stacy had been bringing Basil to the farm every other day so she could supervise the wolf's rehabilitation. She had pored over every book they had in the cave trying to find information on recovery time for lightning-strike-related injuries, but they seemed very rare and often fatal for humans. Basil had been lucky to survive, but Stacy and the pack were definitely in uncharted territory when it came to overseeing her recuperation.

Stacy looked up to see Basil crouching beside her, which meant Basil had walked around the little farm fifteen times.

"Already?" Stacy asked incredulously. "See, I knew you were getting stronger."

Stacy climbed on Basil's back, sitting sidesaddle and sinking her fingers into the wolf's thick white pelt.

"Okay, girl," she said. "Five times around with just me and then five times with me and Page and whatever else I can find to add some more weight."

Basil nodded and began walking at a pretty brisk pace.

"Nice!" Stacy exclaimed excitedly. It felt good to be riding Basil again. Stacy closed her eyes and took a deep breath, filling her lungs with the cool autumn air. Fall was her favorite season and she couldn't wait to eat pumpkin pie, pumpkin soup, pumpkin bread, and, her favorite snack, toasted pumpkin seeds.

A few minutes later, Everest returned with Droplet and Splat. Stacy could only imagine how confusing it must be for the wolf pups to see Stacy sitting on top of Basil holding a pumpkin with Page balanced on top.

"How did it go?" Stacy asked as Page jumped off the pumpkin and began playing with Droplet and Splat. "Did they do okay with the scent drill?"

Everest nodded and then gave Stacy what was left from his training exercise with the pups: a rabbit's foot.

"Um, thanks, I guess," Stacy said, holding the pumpkin in place on her lap with one hand so she could take the rabbit's foot with the other. She tucked it into her satchel. "Actually, I read somewhere these are lucky, but you didn't know that . . . did you?"

Stacy looked down at Everest, waiting for some kind of answer from him, but the huge white wolf only blinked his silver eyes. They were interrupted by a high-pitched warning bark from Page.

Stacy's eyes searched the farm until they found Page, sitting at the entrance to the clearing, her ears twitching wildly. She was listening to something that neither Stacy nor the wolves could hear.

She barked again.

"All right, Page," Stacy said, hopping off Basil and looking back to Everest. "Sounds like Milo will be here any minute."

THREE

STACY SAID GOOD-BYE to Droplet and Splat, who were already falling asleep again, then shimmied through the passageway that separated the farm from the rest of the forest, with Everest, Basil, and Page behind her. They emerged just in time to see Wink happily running toward them. Flying just above him was a small bat . . . Milo.

When Stacy had learned over the summer that Page could communicate with bats, it had changed everything. Now, instead of patrolling the forest and looking for animals that might need rescuing, Stacy and the pack relied on a network of bats to bring them word of animals across the taiga that needed saving. It was a much more efficient system, and Milo was the bat who usually brought the news to Page. In fact, he'd even taken to sleeping in the cave with them on occasion.

Milo hovered above Page for a moment. Then Page took off, running west. Everest and Wink followed behind her.

"Thanks for the rescue tip, Milo," Stacy said, saluting the tiny bat. "You probably can't understand me, so I'm just talking to myself in the forest now. Um, you have a nice day, though."

Milo fluttered off toward the cave and Stacy turned to face Basil.

"All right, girl," Stacy said. "This is your first rescue since the lightning strike. Are you up for it?"

Basil nodded eagerly and Stacy and the wolf set off after the group. They ran for just over a mile until they caught up with the others at the edge of the taiga. Just ahead was a small electrical substation that fed power to the nearby village. Stacy had seen the substation before, but now there was a trailer parked near it, with a large logo on its side that read *Village Construction Co.* Stacy didn't see or hear any people, but her first instinct was to protect her wolves.

"Guys, stay back," she whispered. "Let Page and me scout this one."

Everest, Basil, and Wink obeyed Stacy's command and quietly sank back into the bushes while Stacy and Page emerged from the brush to take a look around.

The front of the trailer seemed to be deserted. They walked around to the back, and Stacy peered through a window. Inside were two dark-haired men—workers from the construction company, she guessed—with their heads close together in conversation. With a gasp, Stacy quickly ducked out of sight, pressing her back against the side of the trailer. She was tempted to slip back into the woods and get as far away from the humans as possible. But then she saw the animal they were meant to be rescuing.

"Oh dear," Stacy whispered, wishing it were actually a deer that needed rescuing . . . or a squirrel or fox or pine marten or anything other than this.

Directly in front of her, trapped in a rectangular wire cage, was a porcupine.

Stacy looked at the garbage cans next to the trailer, then back at the traps, and put two and two together.

"Ugh," she sighed. "Instead of carrying their trash

out with them when they leave for the night, they set traps for the animals who are just looking for a meal. Humans." She felt a surge of anger toward the two men in the trailer behind her.

Page stared up at her blankly. She couldn't really understand what Stacy was talking about, but she was smart enough to stay away from the porcupine. She kept a safe amount of space between her and the spiky creature.

"All right, Everest," Stacy said softly. She knew her wolves' hearing was good enough that they could hear her. "You and Wink can come out. But stay low and quiet. Basil should stay there in case we have to make a run for it."

Everest and Wink slunk through the long grass over to where Stacy and Page were standing. Everest stopped at Stacy's feet, waiting for her next command. Wink, on the other hand, kept going toward the porcupine.

"We'll have to thank Milo for this lovely rescue mission . . . WINK, STOP!" Stacy said as loudly as she dared. The curious wolf had stuck his nose through the cage mesh, sniffing at the frightened porcupine. But it was too late. Wink gave a sudden pained yelp.

"Shh!" Stacy froze as she heard movement from the trailer behind her.

"What was that?" a voice asked, and heavy footsteps came toward the back of the trailer.

"Get down!" Stacy whispered, gesturing frantically to Wink. The wolf turned toward her with a face full of quills and, whining softly, crouched down in the long grass. Stacy ducked below the window and Everest and Page pressed against her. Stacy's heart pounded.

Don't come out here, she thought. She didn't think the man would be able to see them from the window, but if he came out of the trailer, he would be between them and the safety of the woods.

The footsteps stopped by the trailer's window. Stacy held her breath.

There was silence for a moment, then the man said, "Nothing out there," and Stacy heard his footsteps retreat. She stayed still, her hand on Page's back to keep the little dog quiet, and waited until she heard the scrape of the man's chair as he sat down at the table again. Then she hurried toward Wink.

"Oh, Wink!" Stacy exclaimed in a whisper, looking at the sharp quills dotted across the wolf's muzzle. "Poor thing, run home so Tucker can tend to you right away."

She watched as Wink hurried away, holding her breath as he passed the trailer. He got to the woods without the men noticing. *I hope they stay where they are until we're done,* Stacy thought, and bent to examine the trap.

The porcupine inside let out a high-pitched growl and backed away as far as it could, the quills on its back bristling. *He's so scared,* Stacy thought. *Why can't humans leave the animals of the taiga alone?*

"It's okay," she said, trying to sound as soothing as possible. "We're going to help you." Her soft voice seemed to have an effect; after a moment, the porcupine's quills lowered.

Now that the porcupine had calmed, Stacy looked more closely at the trap. It was a big rectangular cage with one side—*the door,* she realized—slanting in toward the porcupine. There was a latch on the top.

I think this will work. Stacy pushed down the latch and used her other hand to raise the slanted side of the cage so that it pressed against the cage roof, leaving an opening. Her hand almost brushed the porcupine's head.

"It's okay," she murmured. "It's okay." *I really hope he doesn't get scared enough to poke me with his quills.*

The porcupine didn't bristle, but he didn't move toward the opening, either. "Don't be scared," Stacy whispered. "Come out." She glanced nervously back at the trailer. They couldn't stay here too long. If the men came out, they'd see them.

The porcupine took a tiny step forward, then hesitated, looking nervously from Stacy to Page. Something nudged Stacy's side. Looking around, she saw Everest holding a long stick in his mouth.

"Good idea," she whispered. Taking the stick in one hand, she maneuvered it through the mesh at the top of the cage, so that it supported the cage door against the ceiling. Once the stick was in place, she let go and took several steps back. Everest and Page backed away, too. The stick held the door open.

The porcupine cautiously poked his head out of the trapdoor and looked around, then took one step out of the cage, then another. Gaining confidence, he turned and quickly trotted away.

Stacy watched the porcupine scamper off into the woods and then turned to see Everest carrying the metal cage in his teeth, toward the river.

"Good idea, boy," Stacy said approvingly. "Maybe they'll learn not to trap animals when they're in their own home."

FOUR

STACY LOOKED DOWN at the steaming bowl of fish porridge in front of her.

"Fish . . . for breakfast, Noah?" Stacy questioned. All of the wolves looked up enthusiastically from their respective wooden bowls. They were obviously enjoying Noah's creation.

Stacy ate a spoonful out of politeness, dumped the remaining portion into Page's bowl while Noah's back was turned, and promptly rooted around the cave's cupboards for some jam and bread.

A couple days had passed since the porcupine rescue,

and the pack had eaten all the pumpkin they'd brought back to the cave that day and made quick work of Addison's pie. Stacy thought it best to lie low for a few days in case any construction workers were trying to find their trap. That's why the group's breakfast consisted of fish that Noah had caught during his patrol a few nights before.

Stacy was still rooting around for something better to eat when Addison entered the cave, back from her turn as the night patrol. She was carrying a newspaper from the village in her mouth. It wasn't unusual for Addison to bring a paper home with her after her patrol shift. But today, instead of neatly placing it on the rocking chair for Stacy to read at her leisure, she angrily spat it from her mouth onto the floor where Stacy was standing.

Stacy bent down to pick up the paper and gasped. There, on the front page, staring straight back at her, was Wink.

Stacy couldn't believe what she was seeing. *Why is Wink's photo in the village newspaper? When (and for that matter, how) was this photo even taken?* The wolves, all finished with their fish porridge, gathered around the table as Stacy read the accompanying article aloud.

ARCTIC WOLF SPOTTED IN NEARBY TAIGA FOREST

A tourist has captured a photo of what appears to be an Arctic wolf in the taiga forest east of the village during July's forest fire.

Lydia Summers, an amateur photographer, was visiting the forest the weekend the blaze broke out, and documented the firefighters' efforts to extinguish the fire.

Several months later, as she was deleting files to make room for new photos, she noticed something she hadn't spotted before. In the background of one of her photos, a white wolf is visible.

"I almost didn't see him," Summers said over the phone. "But he's there, all right. Staring right back at me too, and . . . winking."

Based on the wolf's apparent coloring and size, experts say this is an Arctic wolf—a type of wolf that has never been documented before in this territory, which is generally home to timber wolves.

"I'm ninety-nine percent sure that's an Arctic wolf," said Dr. Wyatt Berg, an area wolf expert and the chair of the Department of Animal Sciences at Village State University. "What an Arctic wolf is doing this far south is unclear, but my students and I intend to find out."

Berg is currently planning a field trip to the forest in hopes of finding and observing the wolf, which he tells us could belong to a larger pack.

This marks the second wolf sighting near the village this year. The first was last spring, when a wolf bounty was instituted due to timber wolves killing farmers' livestock. Local experts believe the forest fire forced those wolves to relocate, and the bounty was lifted in August.

The new wolf sighting will be discussed as an item at this week's village council meeting on October 14.

"Well, great," Stacy muttered. "Wink's famous."

Stacy set down the paper and began pacing around the cave. She looked around at the other wolves. Everest looked angrier than Stacy had ever seen him. His lip was curled up and he glared fiercely at Wink, who was still staring in bewilderment at his picture in the paper. Tucker and Basil had retreated to the cave entrance to keep watch, both looking nervous and alert. Noah was feeding an eager Page her second portion of fish porridge. And Addison was looking at Stacy, waiting to hear what she was going to say.

This is bad, Stacy thought to herself. *We've always had*

to be careful not to be spotted by campers, but, before this, we had the element of surprise on our side. No one expects to see an Arctic wolf here, so even if they did catch a glimpse of one of them, they might not realize what they had seen. But now. . . now they know to be on the lookout for white wolves. Stacy knew she couldn't let the pack see how worried she was.

"Okay, everyone," Stacy began slowly. "Let's focus on the positive. The wolf bounty is over. Yes, it's still hunting season, so we still need to be careful, but no one should be hunting wolves anymore!"

Stacy looked around at the wolves, expecting some excited tail wagging. Instead, they looked relieved but still slightly concerned—expressions Stacy realized were more realistic for when someone tells you that hunters aren't actively trying to kill you anymore.

"All right," Stacy continued. "Second, the article didn't mention building a ski slope or golf course or any type of vacation resort. That's good, right? In fact, it might buy us some time if people are looking for this 'elusive white wolf' in the forest instead of starting construction. Of course, we'll have to make sure they don't find any. . . ."

Stacy's voice trailed off and she resumed pacing around the cave as the wolves settled down for their midmorning nap, their tails low with worry. So many thoughts were racing through her mind. And so many questions, too. There was one thing she was absolutely certain of, though.

She was going to that meeting.

FIVE

"I'M GOING TO the campground to look for more clothes," Stacy announced on a particularly chilly afternoon about a week after she'd read the newspaper article. "And I think it's best if I go alone. There will be a lot of tourists this time of year to see the fall leaves."

Stacy hated lying to her wolves. She almost never did it. But she knew they would never approve if they knew the real reason she wanted to sneak away for a few hours.

Her excuse wasn't a complete lie. She did need some new clothes. She'd grown two inches taller in the last year (Addison had helped her keep track of her height on the cave wall with chalk), and she'd outgrown the few winter clothes she had. It wasn't a bad idea to head over to the campground in the taiga to check out the lost-and-found box or see if anyone had left a jacket or sweatshirt lying around under one of the picnic tables.

But the real reason she wanted to leave the cave for a few hours alone was to go to the village council meeting. Stacy didn't know what she would hear at the meeting, but she knew she had to be there to figure out how to best protect her wolves.

"And don't be alarmed if I'm not back before it gets dark," she said, waving good-bye to the wolves and Page. "People might not get their coats out of their packs until the sun goes down."

Everest shot her a disapproving look.

"Don't worry, boy," Stacy called back to him. "I'll only swipe someone's jacket if I see them littering!"

As soon as Stacy was a few hundred feet away from the cave, she stopped and began furiously combing her hair with her fingers.

"I've got to look civilized," she muttered to herself, tying her hair into a neat side braid with a short piece of vine. She used her tongue to check if she had any blackberry seeds stuck in her teeth, then smoothed out her shirt and tucked it into her pants. *I think this is as civilized as I get.*

It didn't take Stacy long to reach the river that separated the taiga from the village outskirts. There was a bridge, farther to the south near the electrical substation, but Stacy knew of a crossing that was a straight shot to the center of the village. A few nimble jumps across some rocks and she'd crossed the river and set off toward the small town.

She waited in an alley near the village council building while a steady stream of villagers walked past her and entered through the doors. A few minutes after the last villager had gone in, Stacy quietly walked in and took a seat at the back of the large assembly room.

So far, so good, she thought to herself. *I don't think anyone paid me much attention. I can listen to what everyone has to say and then make a run for it when it's over.*

Stacy sat in the uncomfortable metal folding chair for over an hour as villagers took turns talking to the council members about various topics such as crop irrigation, an upcoming election, and funding for new computers at the village library.

It was interesting to Stacy to hear the villagers speaking passionately about the things they believed would make their community better. She didn't know there were humans like this other than the ones she'd met in the woods last summer, Miriam and Jack, who also thought that developing the taiga into a golf course and resort was a terrible idea. The people at the village council reminded Stacy of Miriam as they spoke about different initiatives to improve life in the village, ranging from help for the homeless to better pay for the teachers at the village public school.

Even though the subjects were fascinating to Stacy, the villagers all had rather monotonous voices. She started to catch herself nodding off a few times and looked around to see if anyone had seen her jerk her head up. Luckily, no one was watching her.

"All right, we can now move on to the last topic on the agenda," one of the female villagers seated at the table in the front of the room said in a dry tone. "Would anyone like to discuss the photograph of the Arctic wolf printed in the *Village Gazette* last week?"

Stacy surveyed the room as villagers began whispering to one another in hushed tones.

"I think the photo was a fake. Like the Loch Ness Monster."

"It could just be a white wolf, it doesn't mean it's an Arctic one."

"I take my kids out camping in that forest. It's not safe now."

"They better not start eating my sheep again."

"Shouldn't have ended the wolf bounty so soon."

"Maybe we should have let that forest fire burn a little longer."

Stacy couldn't believe what she was hearing. These were the same villagers who ten minutes ago had been proposing thoughtful plans to improve their town and homes. How could they not understand that the taiga was the wolves' home and they had every right to live there undisturbed?

"I'd like to say something about it, Madam Councilwoman," said a woman standing at the front of the room. Stacy let out a tiny gasp when she saw who was speaking.

It was Miriam.

"In light of the white wolf sighting over the summer, shouldn't the construction company hold off on doing any more work in the forest until it's determined if the forest is home to more of these wolves?"

Stacy smiled. She was so happy to have an ally in the fight against the resort. Like her, Miriam viewed the

taiga as a special place—a place that needed to be protected, not cleared to make way for a golf course.

"I'm not convinced the photo is real," a villager piped up from the back near Stacy. "Even if it was, how do we know that wasn't a lone wolf, just passing through?"

Stacy desperately wanted to speak up. To tell everyone that Wink wasn't a lone wolf. That there were actually six Arctic wolves living in the taiga and they weren't just passing through, it was their home. Not only was it their home, they were a vital part of the taiga's ecosystem and they had humanlike intelligence and they went on rescue missions and . . . *I can't say anything. They probably won't believe me, and if they did, it could put my wolves in danger.*

"Thank you, Ms. Locklear," the councilwoman said to Miriam. "We'll table the discussion until the next meeting."

Stacy snapped back from her thoughts to see that Miriam had sat back down and the meeting was wrapping up. Stacy's plan had been to sneak out early and head back to the forest, but she had a question—and she knew she wouldn't get another opportunity like this one again.

Stacy walked up to Miriam and tapped her on the

shoulder. Miriam turned around and a wave of recognition crept across her face.

"Stacy!" she exclaimed, bringing Stacy close to her for a hug. Stacy had never experienced a hug from a person before. At least, not one that she could remember. Tucker gave amazing hugs, but this hug felt nice, too. And much less hairy.

"It's so nice to see you again," Miriam continued. "Are your parents here?"

Stacy hesitated. *Would a normal human girl come to a council meeting alone?* she wondered. "My family's outside," she said at last. *That's true, anyway. They're all the way back in our cave.*

"Oh, okay," Miriam said. Her eyes narrowed a little, as if she wasn't quite sure Stacy was telling the truth. "I just thought I'd come and lend my voice to try to buy the forest a little more time from the developers."

"It's a really good idea," Stacy said. "I wondered, actually . . . if there was a way to *prove* that there was a pack of Arctic wolves living in the forest, do you think they would cancel the plans to tear it down?"

"I think there's a good chance they'd have to if that was the case," Miriam said. "A pack of wolves like that would need to be studied. The local college would probably be able to secure government funding to do research. The National Park Service might even be interested in protecting the land."

"Protecting the land?" Stacy queried. "What does that mean?"

"Sometimes the government will designate an area of land as a national park or forest because of its geology or historical significance . . . or, in this case, because it's home to a certain rare species of wildlife," Miriam told her. "Arctic wolves aren't endangered, luckily. But they're not found this far south, so they would be considered rare for this part of the world and their habitat worth protecting. But that's provided there really is a pack of Arctic wolves living in the forest here, which seems like a long shot."

Stacy looked down in disbelief. She knew her wolves were the protectors and guardians of the taiga, but it had never occurred to her that they could be the key to saving it altogether. If only there was a way to show everyone that the pack lived there, without all the attention that would follow.

"You've never seen a white wolf while you were out . . . camping, have you?" Miriam asked her.

"No, I haven't," Stacy lied, looking up to meet Miriam's gaze. *Wow, two lies in one day. This is a new low for me.* "But I'll keep an eye out if I do go camping again."

"That's fine, but please be careful," Miriam cautioned. "Wolves will usually keep their distance from humans, but remember they're wild."

"Oh, I know they're wild," Stacy said.

It was all she could do not to smile.

SIX

THE FOLLOWING MORNING, Stacy was at the farm with Everest, Basil, and Tucker. Basil was doing her laps while Tucker groomed Droplet and Splat, much to their dismay. Stacy and Everest stood just out of earshot of the others (or at least, Stacy hoped it was out of earshot). They were supposed to be gathering kindling and mushrooms, but really Stacy was brainstorming ways they could get the taiga designated as protected land. She had confided to Everest her real motivation for leaving the cave the night before.

"We need a camera," Stacy said to Everest. "If I were to take pictures of the pack and give them to Miriam, then she could show them to whoever is in charge of national parks."

Everest gave a sharp yip. Stacy knew he was still mad at her for lying about where she was going last night, but she went on anyway.

"The problem is," Stacy continued, "what do I tell Miriam when she asks how I got the photos? Maybe I take them from really far away and I can say that I spotted you on a hike? Or maybe I give her the photos and run away before she has a chance to ask me, that could work."

Everest looked back at her again and huffed in frustration.

"Yes, there's still the issue of how I get a camera," Stacy said excitedly. "I've had a few thoughts. From what I know about cameras, I can't exactly ask to borrow one from a camper. I'd have to take the little memory chip thingy to give to Miriam, and that would mean stealing something really valuable from someone. We can't do that. So, hear me out, Everest. What if I were to get a part-time job in the village? Washing dishes or something simple like that—only to make enough money to buy a cheap camera . . ."

Everest let out a loud growl—more of a roar, really. He was definitely not a fan of her idea.

"All right, boy, don't worry," Stacy said, patting his thick fur. "We'll think of something else."

A few minutes later, Stacy waved good-bye to Droplet and Splat, who, thanks to Tucker, looked a hundred times cleaner than when they arrived. Stacy set off toward the cave with Basil, Everest, and Tucker walking beside her. Normally, Stacy stayed very alert when she was walking through the forest with her wolves. But with Basil getting stronger every day and Everest by her side, she allowed her mind to wander.

We got enough mushrooms to make a stew for dinner. It's not my favorite meal, and the wolves won't touch it, but it's better than fish porridge, that's for sure. It can't just be a mushroom stew, though; I'll have to add something else to thicken it up. Beetroot, maybe? Or apples? Do apples go well with mushrooms?

Stacy had just decided on adding wild leeks when Everest, Basil, and Tucker suddenly veered off course, ducking behind some large, mossy boulders.

"What's going—"

"Stacy!" a male voice called out.

Stacy spun around to see Jack, the man who had been camping with Miriam over the summer. Stacy recognized him instantly. She didn't have many conversations with humans, so the ones she had were fairly memorable. But more important, she remembered him because Jack had told her what s'mores were.

Ever since that conversation, Stacy couldn't get the gooey dessert out of her mind. She'd even dreamt about them and how they would taste—marshmallow-filled, melty daydreams that she had while staring at her large bowl of fish porridge.

"Hi, Jack," Stacy answered as Jack jogged to meet her where she was standing. "What are you doing off-trail?"

"Could ask you the same question," Jack replied with a wink. "Miriam and I were on a hike, but I brought my good camera so I thought I'd head off-trail for a bit and see if I could snap a photo of one of those white wolves everyone's talking about."

Stacy looked down at the sturdy camera that hung around Jack's neck.

"Had any luck?" Stacy asked nervously. *Had Jack already seen us out walking?*

"Not yet," Jack said, much to Stacy's relief. "I was just about to get my binoculars out, though, to see if I could spot one." Jack gently took the camera from around his neck and set it on a nearby boulder. Next, he took off the backpack he was wearing and brought it around to his stomach, balancing it on his bent knee so he could open it. He fished out a large pair of binoculars and set the backpack on the ground at the base of the boulder the camera was resting on.

"I'm going to get a little higher—maybe I'll see something," he said, and began to scramble up a rock pile to where he had a decent vantage point over part of the taiga. He pressed the binoculars to his eyes and scanned the horizon. "Or at least see where Miriam wandered off to."

Without any warning, a flash of white encircled Stacy. Whatever it was, it grazed her, knocking her a little off-balance. She rocked back and forth on her feet and stumbled backward, catching herself on the boulder where the camera was. But the camera wasn't there. It was gone.

"JACK," Stacy yelled. "Your camera!"

Jack scrambled down the rock rubble to where Stacy was standing. She was still rattled from whatever had brushed by her on the trail a few moments ago.

"What happened?" he asked when he'd reached the bottom. "Are you all right?"

"I'm fine," Stacy said. "But your camera . . . I saw something move in the bushes and then—it . . . it was gone. I don't know what happened. I'm sorry!"

"Probably a raccoon!" Jack said with disgust as he began looking around the boulder. "He couldn't have dragged it far."

"It might have gone that way," Stacy said, pointing in the opposite direction from where she knew Everest, Basil, and Tucker were crouching. "I'll keep an eye out too, and come back here if I find it, but I'd better be going. Good luck!"

Before Jack could ask her any more questions, Stacy slipped into the trees and zigzagged away from Jack, knowing the wolves would find a safe way to catch up to her without being seen.

Sure enough, after about three minutes of walking silently through the forest, Everest suddenly appeared beside Stacy. Next, Tucker came bounding up behind her. And then Stacy saw Basil. Basil was in front of Stacy and holding something in her teeth. The camera.

"Basil, you found it!" Stacy said eagerly, running up to her. Basil looked down in shame and Stacy remembered the white flash.

"You . . . you stole it?" she said incredulously. "How?"

Tucker walked up to Basil and looped his head through the camera strap Basil had clenched in her teeth. At the same time, Everest used his big body to back Stacy up against a tree. He nodded for her to stay still and then looked back to Basil expectantly.

Suddenly, Basil was gone. Stacy blinked and looked around and noticed the same white blur weaving in and out through the trees. It was Basil. She was sprinting so quickly Stacy's eyes could barely keep up with where she was going.

And then Basil was back standing in front of Stacy and the others, panting heavily and waiting for Stacy's reaction.

"You were never that fast before the lightning strike," Stacy whispered as she took a step toward Basil and ran her hand down her back. She didn't know what to think. Had the lightning given Basil some special ability?

Tucker walked over and bowed his head, indicating that Stacy should take the camera that was around his neck.

"Okay," Stacy began, taking the camera from Tucker and trying to put together the pieces of what had just transpired. "Basil, you must have overheard Everest's and my discussion of why we need a camera. And it was you who took the camera from the boulder, not a raccoon, thanks to your new . . . um, super speed?"

Tucker nodded enthusiastically, while Everest beamed with pride. Basil gave Stacy one nod, still waiting to know if she was in trouble or not.

"I'm not mad, Basil," Stacy said. "I'm just . . . concerned. Let's go home. We'll take some pictures of you and the rest of the wolves tomorrow and figure out a way to get this back to Jack. But for now, I want you to rest."

Stacy and the wolves set off back toward the cave, taking a slightly longer route to avoid passing through any clearings. They could stay safe in the shadows of the towering spruce trees. Stacy felt a weight around her neck that wasn't just the heavy camera. She was worried about what she'd seen Basil do. It worried her because, deep down, she knew it wasn't supposed to be possible.

The wolves had always been special. They took in a lost human girl—they could understand her commands and help to rescue small animals they'd usually hunt. But Basil's swiftness was not the same as exceptional intelligence and an unusual diet. It was superhuman speed. Or in Basil's case, superwolf speed. And Stacy didn't know what to make of it.

SEVEN

"ALL RIGHT, WHO'S ready to have their picture taken?" Stacy said to the pack, standing at the hearth in the cave the following morning. Page began twirling in front of her, looking at the camera in Stacy's hands as if it were a piece of meat.

"Sorry, Page," Stacy said. "This camera is not edible, and you do not need your picture taken."

She turned to the wolves, who were finishing their breakfast—fish, raw egg, and pumpkin.

"Now I know it's a risk to photograph all of you," she began. "But it's the best chance we have of saving the forest and keeping our home. And to make sure they don't find our cave, I propose we take the photos in a part of the taiga we hardly ever go to. I was thinking the Forest of Perpetual Darkness."

All of the wolves' ears perked up. Addison's jaw dropped open, a piece of pumpkin falling back into her wooden bowl.

The Forest of Perpetual Darkness was a particularly gloomy patch of the taiga biome, northwest of their cave. Stacy always got the impression the wolves were somewhat spooked by it, which was strange. She had never known her wolves to be afraid of anything. They had been there in July when they rescued a young moose, but they hadn't been back since.

Everest shook his head, a firm no.

"I know you don't like that part of the taiga," Stacy said. "But that's what makes it perfect. We shouldn't go back there after the photos are seen, because that's where people will be looking for you. After today, we'll never go back there."

All of the wolves seemed to like the idea of never returning after this once. Everest and Addison exchanged glances and both nodded slowly in agreement. It was decided. They were going to the Forest of Perpetual Darkness.

Stacy spent the rest of the morning trying to figure

out how to take pictures on the camera. She had to be quick because she had no way to charge the camera should the battery run low. She taught herself how to focus the lens and take a picture and how to view the picture and delete it.

They walked north for about an hour before veering a little west, where they began to climb into the low hills that lay at the edge of the dark forest.

Stacy and the wolves had to walk much more slowly inside the dark forest. Their path was crowded with thick scrub oak trees they needed to climb through. Every few steps, they had to completely change direction to avoid a tangle of branches and brush. Progress was extremely slow, and an hour or so later, Stacy decided they'd gone in far enough. But just as she slowed to a stop, Everest and Addison quickened their pace.

"Hold on," Stacy called out. "I think this area will work fine!"

Everest motioned for the group to keep going.

"Ever," Stacy said, slightly annoyed. "No one is going to be able to tell north from south in any photo we take here if you're worried about someone tracking us back to our cave. But the scrub oak trees are a dead giveaway that we're in the dark forest, and that big patch of podzol over there proves this is still in the taiga. It's perfect. Let's just take the pictures here so we can get home before it gets dark."

Relenting, Everest circled back to where Stacy was standing with the other wolves. He nudged her, hurrying her along.

"Okay," Stacy said, putting her arms around Wink and Noah as if they were a huddling sports team. "All of you need to be in the photo, because the more Arctic wolves there are, the better the chance they'll want to protect the land as your habitat. So, spread out, but don't go so far that you go out of the camera frame."

Wink and Noah ran off in front of Stacy and began digging in the soft podzol. Tucker and Basil both decided to lie down and rest. Stacy wasn't sure if it was for the photos or if they were just tired from the journey there. Addison and Everest awkwardly stood side by side on Stacy's left. They seemed restless and uneasy.

"Back up, you two," she said, waving them away from the lens. They each took a few steps back but maintained their strange posture.

"It's too posed," Stacy said with one eye squinting into the camera viewfinder. "Act natural. Act like you're a pack. Like you're a pack of Arctic wolves just living your life in the taiga."

Stacy lifted her head above the camera and saw that all the wolves were staring blankly at her.

"Right," she said. "Okay, that was a dumb thing to say. Just be yourselves and don't look at the camera."

Stacy peered back into the viewfinder and took a few photos.

"Except Wink," she called out. "Wink, I want you to look at me and do that winking thing with your eye so it's clear that you're the wolf from the original photo."

Stacy took about thirty photos, including some close-ups of the individual wolves, and then quickly turned the camera off to conserve the battery.

"Okay, we got it!" she said triumphantly. "You all did amazing for your first photo shoot. Now let's go home."

Later that night, Stacy sat in her rocking chair with Page on her lap, scrolling through the photos on the camera. She wanted to make sure the wolves looked like "wild" wolves in all of the pictures. She wasn't sure yet how she planned to get the camera back to Jack; she still needed to figure that out.

As she cycled through the photos, she stopped on one of Addison and Everest. Everest had a strange expression in this one, as if he was looking back at someone, or something, behind him. *Of course, I should have directed* some of them to look slightly nervous, since they're supposed to look like they're being spied on, not posing for the photos. *Good thinking, Everest. But what was he looking at?* Stacy zoomed in on the photo, particularly on a large tree in the distance that was covered with vines. There was something in the tree . . . it looked like . . .

Stacy couldn't believe it. It looked like a helicopter blade. What would a helicopter be doing in the forest?

With a chill, she realized: *Addison and Everest knew this was there and they didn't tell me. Why?*

She thought about how quickly they'd agreed to stop instead of going farther into the forest, and how reluctant they'd been to go there in the first place. *They're hiding something from me,* Stacy realized.

"Oof, Addi," Stacy said, startled, as Addison plopped a book on Stacy's lap next to Page. "What's this?"

Stacy held the book up, an old atlas they'd salvaged from the dumpster behind the village library, and looked at the page it was open to. It was the last page of a section about the National Parks of the United States of America. *Okay, I'm thinking Addison can definitely read.* On the bottom of the page there was an address for the National Parks Service, as well as the U.S. Forest Service at the Department of Agriculture.

"Addi, this is it!" Stacy said excitedly. "This address

and book are probably older than me, but it's worth a try."

She turned the camera over and ejected the memory card, like she'd seen tourists do in the past.

"We'll send this to the Forest Service, along with a letter about the wolves, and that way we don't have to explain to Jack how we took the photos." She felt bad about taking Jack's memory card, but he had been hoping to get photos of the wolves for just this purpose anyway. *If he knew, he would be glad to use his memory card for this.*

Page jumped down to the ground as Stacy stood up from her rocking chair and walked over to where she kept her journal and ink and quill. She turned to the back of the leather-bound journal and carefully tore out a page. Using the ink and quill, she scribbled a quick note about how the memory card contained photos of an Arctic wolf pack, along with the coordinates to the taiga, which she and Addison had deduced several summers ago from their world atlas.

Stacy placed the memory card from the camera in the center of her note and folded the paper into an envelope, something she'd learned from an origami book she had in the cave. She addressed the envelope to the U.S. Forest Service c/o the Bureau of Federal Land Management.

Next, she rummaged through an old ammo container she had filled with little odds and ends she'd collected while walking in the forest over the years, searching for some postage for the letter.

"I know I've found stamps before," Stacy said, sifting through the layers of coins, fishing lures, lighters, and pocket knives. She glanced up from the container and something silver caught her eye, glinting from one of the shelves of her bookcase.

It was the charm bracelet Everest had given her for her rescue day. Stacy picked it up, letting the chain run between her fingers, and looked at the charms. A horse, a helicopter, a book, the letter S, a mermaid. She twisted the little helicopter between two fingers. It made her think of the helicopter blade in the picture from the dark forest. Why did both those things give her a strange, hollow feeling in her chest, as if she had forgotten something very important?

"Addi?" Stacy asked. "Do you know where Everest found this bracelet?" She looked down, but Addison was avoiding her eyes. Instead, the graceful wolf nosed at the ammo container.

Stacy looked down again and saw what she had been looking for: an old roll of postcard stamps with little hummingbirds on them. She turned around to see

Addison standing at her desk with her tongue out.

"Why, thank you, Addi," Stacy said, ripping a stamp from the roll and pressing it to Addison's tongue and then onto the envelope. "We better add two, just in case."

It was Addison's turn to patrol the ridge that night, which worked out perfectly. Under the cover of night, Stacy and Addison snuck into the village and mailed the letter.

Stacy climbed on top of Addison so she could look down into the metal mailbox.

"Looks like it fell to the bottom," Stacy whispered to Addison, who was peering up at her inquisitively. "Fingers crossed this works."

Stacy carefully climbed off Addison and the two set off back toward the forest.

"I should have included a name suggestion," Stacy said as she and Addison slipped back into the trees. "Stacy's Taiga."

Addison rolled her eyes and gave Stacy a playful nudge.

"Oh, you don't like that, girl?" Stacy said, wrapping her arms around Addison's neck and hugging her as they walked. "Okay, let's see . . .

"Mount Stacy National Park . . .

"Addison's Acres . . .

"Stacy and Addison's National Forest . . .

"Fine, Addison and Stacy's National Forest."

Stacy's voice disappeared into the sound of the swaying taiga trees that enveloped them as they made their way back to the cave by the light of the stars.

EIGHT

THE SUN WAS just beginning to peek through the mega spruce trees that surrounded their cave as Stacy set out the next morning. Stacy had told the wolves she was going to meet Addison as the wolf was coming off her patrol duty, but that was another lie. She was going to the Forest of Perpetual Darkness to look for the helicopter. If her wolves were hiding something from her, she wanted to know what it was.

Without a wolf to ride, it took Stacy several hours to make her way back to the spot where they had taken the photos. The sun was directly overhead as Stacy entered the dark forest. She knew Addison would be back by now and the wolves would have discovered she and Addison had never met up. They might be looking for her right now. But she kept going. This felt like her only chance to find out the truth.

Finally, Stacy pushed her way through a last tangle of brush and saw the wreckage in front of her. It looked like the skeleton of a helicopter. There had been a fire: the metal of the helicopter and the branches around it were charred and black. The glass was gone from the windows. She moved closer, examining it. The helicopter must have fallen through the trees, she realized—there were broken branches and felled trees beneath it—but it had been there long enough that more trees and bushes had grown over and around it.

The front of the helicopter was crushed and blackened, but the back was almost whole. Stacy stepped up on a fallen log and peered in. Fire had destroyed the front seats, she saw at a glance. There were a few white bones among the ashes, and Stacy felt sick at the sight. Humans had died here.

The back seat was still intact. There were the remains of a brightly colored book there, its pages pulpy and unreadable from the rains that had fallen since the helicopter had crashed. Beside it was a half-destroyed, moldy shape that Stacy recognized as a stuffed animal. *A lamb,* she thought, and she reached out a hand to touch it, leaning against the side of the helicopter. There was an alarming creak and the helicopter shifted. Stacy stepped back.

There was something familiar about the stuffed lamb. Just like there was something familiar about the bracelet. The bracelet that Everest had brought her, without wanting to tell her where it came from.

This is how I came to the forest, Stacy realized. She was sure of it. She looked again at the charred and crushed front of the helicopter. *No one could have survived in there.*

My parents are dead.

Stacy heard a branch break and spun around to see Basil, Everest, and Tucker.

"Is this where you found me?" Stacy said, her eyes welling up with tears.

Everest nodded solemnly while Basil hung her head. Tucker ran to Stacy and she threw her arms around him and sobbed into his chest.

Stacy cried for a long time, her face buried in Tucker's thick white fur. He made soft, comforting noises, licking the top of her head, while Basil and Everest pressed their cool noses against her cheeks.

At last, she stopped crying. Her eyes felt sore and itchy,

and she was dragging in long, harsh breaths. While she cried, hot anger had been rising inside her. Her pack had known where she had come from and they had tried to keep her away from the place where they had found her. They had known that her parents were dead.

She sat back on her heels, pushing away from Tucker's chest. Then she got to her feet without looking at any of her wolves. They tried to stand close beside her, but she turned away.

"You should have shown me this sooner," Stacy said, brushing past Everest so that she was ahead of the wolves.

If Stacy had looked into Everest's eyes, she would have been met with a sorrowful expression that said, *I know*. But she trudged past him and set off down the hill.

They walked in silence all the way back to the cave.

NINE

BACK AT THE cave, Stacy walked right past Addison and Noah and took a seat in her rocking chair. She stayed there for the rest of the night.

It was the first time she could ever remember not sleeping next to the wolves. And sleep did not come easy. Stacy might have blamed it on the hard wooden rocking chair—it was difficult to find a comfortable sleeping position—but she was also cycling through a whole range of emotions that kept her from falling asleep.

She felt betrayed by her wolves and angry with Everest. But she was also relieved to finally know how she had wound up lost in the taiga and happy to know there was no one looking for her who would take her from her wolf family. *The wolf family that didn't tell me the truth,* she thought, feeling furious at them all over again. She shifted in the chair and wiped one hand across her wet eyes.

Most of all, Stacy was sad that her parents were dead. She hadn't been abandoned in the woods, hadn't wandered away from an absentminded mom and dad. Her parents had loved her.

This both comforted Stacy and saddened her. She would never know them. Stacy cradled the small charm bracelet in her hand and pulled her arms into her shirt to stay warm. Page stretched out on her lap for the night and Wink curled up at her feet, his warm brown eyes looking up at her anxiously. Stacy knew she could never stay mad at Wink, and besides, he had been only a pup when Stacy had come to live with the wolves. He had been as clueless as Stacy about her origins.

Morning eventually came and Stacy pried herself out of the sturdy rocking chair. She didn't speak to the wolves like she normally would. Instead she silently fixed herself something to eat from the pantry and returned to her chair. Addison nudged her with a peace offering, a slice of pumpkin bread, but Stacy didn't even look up from the book she was reading. After a moment, Addison put the pumpkin bread beside her and walked away, her tail drooping sadly.

Stacy bit her lip. Ignoring Addison was the cruelest thing she'd ever done to her. It wasn't that Stacy wanted to give the wolves the silent treatment, but she honestly didn't know what to say to them. Deep down she knew the wolves had only meant well, but it still felt like a betrayal. So she kept quiet, afraid of saying something she might regret.

Usually at about this time, Stacy would be choosing a wolf to accompany her on whatever outing she had planned for that day, but she didn't feel like going anywhere. So Stacy lost herself in a book instead, and didn't even look up as Noah, Everest, and Basil set out to visit Droplet and Splat.

Several hours passed and Stacy stayed completely immersed in her book. It was a long one, *Journey to the Center of the Earth* by Jules Verne. Stacy had just reached the halfway point when Milo the bat swooped into the cave at breakneck speed. Page jumped off Stacy's lap and ran out of the cave with all the wolves on her heels.

Stacy quickly dog-eared the page of her book she was reading (there was no time to find a bookmark) and hurried after everyone else. She knew it must be an emergency rescue. Usually they would take the time to at least look at the map before leaving the cave so that Page could show them where they were headed. Stacy ran out of the cave into the clearing and gasped.

"Noah!"

Propped up against Everest was a very unsteady Noah. He took a wobbly step forward and then collapsed onto the ground. His eyes closed, and Stacy couldn't tell if he was still breathing.

"What happened to him?" Stacy yelled at Everest, breaking her silence as the alpha ran into the cave. And then she saw it. Sticking out of Noah's shoulder was a small dart.

Did they poison him? Stacy's heart was pounding with panic.

What if the villagers have found my wolves before we've had a chance to make up? She didn't want anything to happen to Noah, especially not while he thought she was angry with him.

Stacy lunged toward the dart and pulled it from Noah's shoulder blade. She quickly ran her hands through his fur, feeling his sides, and then exhaled in relief. He was breathing. *It must have been a tranquilizer dart,* Stacy thought. Noah was unconscious, not dead.

But who shot him with that dart?

"Basil, set up a perimeter!" Stacy said in an urgent, hushed voice. Basil hurried away and disappeared into the trees, off to make sure no one was closing in on their location. Everest returned from the cave with an old ripped tarp they'd found discarded at the campground.

"Good," Stacy said, taking the tarp and spreading it out on the ground. Everest, Tucker, and Addison rolled Noah, who was fast asleep, onto the tarp and each took a corner of it in their mouths. Stacy grabbed tight to the last corner. Together they pulled Noah into the cave while Wink covered up their tracks behind them. Once inside, they positioned Noah in front of the hearth.

Wink attempted in vain to rouse him with his nose while Tucker checked Noah for more darts. Everest was at the cave's entrance, waiting for Basil to return. Stacy looked up to see Addison already at the bookcase, nosing through some medical texts.

"I assume he'll come to in a few hours, Addi," Stacy said, placing the dart down on her desk. She began to thumb through the books, looking for anything about sedation. "We'll keep his mouth open and get some fresh water for when he wakes up, but that's about all we can do."

Suddenly Everest was beside Stacy, his massive body leaning over her, pressing his nose to her lips to stop her from talking. Stacy quieted and then she heard it. Human voices. Coming from outside the cave.

"No sign of the male, Dr. Berg," a young woman's voice called out.

Stacy froze. The voices were very close. She had pulled the branch trapdoor across the cave entrance, but would it disguise the opening well enough? What if the humans had shot Noah with a tracking dart?

Page's ears pricked up in interest at the voices. Silently, Stacy slid a hand over her muzzle, hoping the little dog would stay quiet. Holding her breath, Stacy looked around at her pack. They were all still and silent, their attention fixed on the voices outside the cave.

"He could have run into a cave or behind some boulders," a deeper voice said. "Look carefully for white fur." Stacy stiffened. What would she and the wolves do if the cave was found?

The noise from the footsteps grew louder outside as the humans searched. Finally, the young woman said, "I think he ran farther. He was heading northwest."

The male voice said sharply, "Did you see that?" Pounding footsteps began, as if the humans had broken into a run. In a few moments, the sounds of their footsteps had faded.

Stacy let out a shaky breath, relieved. The researchers were probably being led away by Basil. As much as Basil's newfound speed confused Stacy, she was thankful for it in this moment. *A dozen wolf researchers could try to land a shot on Basil and they'd all miss,* she thought.

The wolves took turns lying near Noah all evening, including Basil who had successfully eluded the researchers and returned to the cave. Stacy never left Noah's side. She wondered how it was possible that just this morning she had been angry with these magnificent creatures she was lucky enough to call family. She ran a hand over the messy tuft of fur between Noah's ears. *What if I'd lost him?*

The wolves hadn't told her the truth. But they had protected her and loved her since her first rescue day. She understood they hadn't wanted to hurt her by showing her something so horrible, something she had forgotten.

The helicopter crash was tragic, but it is in the past, Stacy thought. She squeezed her eyes shut for a moment. It still hurt: her human family was *dead*, and she had forgotten them. *Someday I'll learn more about them,* she promised herself. But right now, the only family she knew was right here in the cave with her. And they needed protecting.

Ordinarily, Stacy would have been thrilled to see conservationists in the taiga. It was definitely the type of work she'd want to be doing if she didn't already have a job rescuing animals. The fact that the research team was searching the forest could mean they were one step closer to getting the forest designated as protected land. But having them tranquilize one of her wolves was a step too far.

How can I protect them from an entire team of researchers who are out here looking for glimpses of white fur?

"Snow," Stacy said quietly under her breath.

Addison's ears perked up and she lifted her head to look at Stacy.

"It's not safe for you here until it snows," Stacy continued, looking around the cave at the others. "You stand out too much. That's why they were able to shoot Noah. Wolves like Droplet and Splat—their markings are suited to the dark foliage of a taiga forest. Addison's got a tinge of brown in her coat that helps a bit, but for the most part, you're all as white as . . . snow."

Stacy stood up to address the group. They were all looking at her now, their ears pricked in interest.

"If today has taught me anything, it's that I need to do whatever it takes to not lose any more of my family. I'm sorry I reacted badly. And I'm sorry for the lies I've told these last few weeks. No more lies. No more leaving without telling you where I'm going. And no more close calls."

Stacy took a deep breath and steadied herself for the reaction she knew would come from her next sentence.

"I think we should leave the taiga and return only after the first snowfall."

The wolves sat in stunned silence. Stacy took this as a good sign. At least they seemed open to the idea. She knew the stress of the wolf bounty and Wink's photo in the paper had been weighing on them. She continued.

"We'd only be gone a few months," Stacy said. "Think of it like a vacation. We can bring Milo, too, and do rescues wherever we go. A proper rescue expedition! By the time we're back, there will be plenty of snow to camouflage all of you and we won't have to worry so much about being seen until it thaws in the spring. It's perfect."

Stacy looked at each of her wolves. Everest, Wink, Addison, Tucker, and Basil stared back at her, all with similar, unsure expressions. Suddenly, an enthusiastic bark rang out from behind Stacy. She spun around to see Noah, awake and standing.

Everyone ran to Noah—Tucker and Basil nuzzling him while Page rubbed her head against one of his legs, looking up at him adoringly.

"That settles it, then," Stacy said with a smile. "We'll leave tomorrow."

TEN

MORNING CAME AND Stacy hadn't slept a wink. Wink, on the other hand, was still sleeping, curled up by the fire next to Page and Noah. Everest was out checking on Droplet and Splat one last time before they left. The young wolves should be old enough now to fend for themselves for a few months.

Tucker had just returned from patrol duty. It had been Noah's turn, but everyone agreed he should get a good night's rest after his brush with the tranquilizer dart. Obviously, Noah didn't need the extra rest. As soon as he saw Stacy was awake he leapt up and greeted her.

"Hiya, boy," Stacy said, taking his head into her hands and scratching behind his ears.

Next Stacy walked over to where Basil and Addison were nestled and bent down to wake them.

"Wake up, sleepyheads," Stacy cooed. "We've still got to winterize the cave and pack some snacks for the trip."

Winterizing the cave was Stacy's fancy way of saying they needed to collect enough dry firewood to keep her warm during the coldest months of the year. If they weren't coming back until after it snowed in the taiga, they'd have to gather the wood now.

"I stayed up all night making some stuff for the journey," Stacy continued as she grabbed a large item from her rocking chair. "May I present to you all . . . the very first prototype of my Wolf Pack Hip Pack!"

Stacy held it up for the wolves to see. She'd taken a pair of khaki cargo pants she'd long outgrown and cut and sewn them into a crude saddlebag with a large pocket on each side. She'd made a very basic pack for the wolves to wear several years ago, but it was completely worn out from years of carrying kindling, apples, and whatever else they found in the forest back to the cave. This new pack had a much more durable design, Stacy was sure of it.

"Noah, I think you should have the honor of wearing it first," Stacy said, draping it over Noah's withers and fastening the button under his belly. Noah puffed up with pride.

"I can't carry everything we need in my satchel," Stacy explained. "This will hold our water canteens, any fish Noah catches, and . . ."

Stacy walked back over to her rocking chair and grabbed another object that was hanging on its back.

"This!" Stacy exclaimed, holding out a large coil of vines from the Forest of Perpetual Darkness. She had knotted and braided them together to form a sturdy rope about thirty feet in length.

"I just thought we should be prepared for anything," she said. "We definitely could have used a rope like this a long time ago, but my knot-tying skills weren't cutting it back then." Tucker sniffed the rope and wagged his tail in approval.

Stacy took the Wolf Pack Hip Pack off of Noah and crammed the rope into one of the side pockets. Next, she emptied the contents of their small, makeshift pantry into the other. It wasn't much, just some apples, dried berries, and a few small loaves of homemade bread.

They spent the rest of the morning gathering firewood,

filling their canteens at the river, and helping Stacy practice her archery with the bow and arrows Tucker had given her on her rescue day. Stacy was getting pretty good with them, hitting the target (a fallen spruce tree) an average of four times out of six. Each time Stacy had shot all six of the arrows, the wolves and Page would run over to retrieve them.

Once they had dragged all the firewood back to the cave and stacked it neatly beside the fireplace, Stacy packed her satchel with a few essentials: a pair of binoculars, her hunting knife, a compass, and all the paper money she'd ever found in the forest, which added up to fifty-two dollars. She wanted to be prepared in case she needed to buy something for the wolves or Page while they were traveling.

Sadly, Stacy realized *Journey to the Center of the Earth* was far too heavy a book to bring with her and she'd have to finish it when they returned. Instead she reached for one of the first books she'd ever read, a thin paperback copy of *The Boxcar Children* by Gertrude Chandler Warner. *This will do nicely,* she thought. *And it's quite appropriate considering where I'm leading everyone.*

The charm bracelet glittered at her from the bookcase shelf. She picked it up and held it in her hand, looking at the charms—the horse, the helicopter. *Did Everest find this in the helicopter?* she wondered. *Is this something my parents gave me?*

Deep inside, she was sure of it. Each of the charms looked even more special to her now. They were tiny links to the parents she couldn't remember. The bracelet was too small to wear on her wrist now, so Stacy rooted around in her box of trinkets until she found a thin strand of leather cording. She carefully slipped the charms off the bracelet and slid them onto the cording, securing it around her neck with slip knots and tucking it into her shirt. *I'll keep them with me,* she promised herself. *Someday, I'll find out about my human family.*

For now, though, she needed to save the family she still had. She looked around at her wolf pack. Tucker was standing guard at the cave entrance. Noah was sprawled by the hearth, warming his belly. Wink and Page were chasing each other playfully around the rocking chair, yipping with excitement. Addison was examining a newspaper in the corner. Everest was still out with the wolf pups, giving them one last hunting lesson. But someone was missing.

"Where's Basil?" Stacy said sharply. Tucker turned his head toward her, then quickly looked away. It was clear to Stacy that he knew where Basil had slipped off to when Stacy wasn't looking.

Stacy frowned in concern. It was important that none of them wandered away, not while the researchers were still searching the forest for the wolves. Before she could ask Tucker again, though, Basil slipped through the cave entrance, her tail high with excitement.

"Where have you been?" Stacy asked. "We're going to leave soon."

Basil came over and pushed her muzzle against Stacy's hand. Stacy turned her hand palm up and Basil dropped something into it. It was a flint and steel from the mines at the edge of the taiga, just like the ones Basil used to build fires in the hearth.

"Is this for me?" Stacy asked, surprised. She had always wanted to learn to build fires like the sleek yellow-eyed wolf did. Basil nodded and pressed her face against Stacy's side.

This is a belated rescue day present, Stacy realized. Basil had still been too injured on rescue day to give Stacy a present, but now she was showing Stacy how glad she was that they were each other's family.

Stacy dropped to her knees, threw her arms around Basil's neck, and hugged her. "You didn't need to get me a present," she told Basil. "But I love it." Basil wagged her tail as Stacy carefully tucked the flint and steel into her satchel.

Getting to her feet, Stacy was looking around the cave one last time for anything she might have forgotten to pack when Everest came in, back from checking up on Droplet and Splat. At the same time, Milo flew into the cave and hung upside down from the ceiling in his favorite spot.

Addison was standing over by the map they'd drawn with chalk on one of the cave walls. Everyone gathered around her.

"Here." Stacy pointed. She placed her finger at the very bottom of the map, the southernmost part of the taiga they'd ever explored. "There's something down here that is going to help us get away from here faster than we can ever manage by foot, er, I mean . . . paw. That's where I want to go."

Stacy and the wolves exited the cave and carefully covered the entrance with branches and stones so it wouldn't be discovered. Stacy hoisted the heavy pack onto Noah and they all headed out, running at a steady pace. They'd traveled about ten miles south before Stacy and Page got tired and needed to hop onto Wink's back.

She snuggled into the wolf's fur as they walked for what Stacy figured must have been another twelve miles or so until they reached them . . . train tracks.

"We're here!" Stacy said, hopping off Wink. A look of terror flashed across Everest's face. He knew what Stacy was planning.

"Come on, Everest," Stacy said. "Where's your sense of adventure? Don't you want to get out of the taiga quickly? It will take us days to get to the next biome otherwise."

After several more minutes of convincing, Everest at last nodded reluctantly, and everyone sat down beside the track to wait for a train. Stacy passed the time by pouring water for everyone in a little wooden bowl she'd brought and then reading her book while the wolves napped.

The sun had just gone down when Page sprang to her feet and began running in circles while Milo fluttered above her. A train was coming. The wolves got up and stretched while Stacy pulled her binoculars out of her bag and looked up and down the tracks.

"It's a northbound!" Stacy said excitedly as the tracks began to rattle. "That's what we want!"

She grabbed her bow and the quiver full of arrows

and slung them around her back. The wolves lined up, ready to jump.

"Wait!" Stacy yelled. The train was closer now and Stacy could just make out the rows and rows of windows with human faces pressed against the glass, taking in the taiga's scenery.

"Observation cars!" Stacy shouted at the top of her lungs. "HIDE!"

Stacy and the wolves (and Page and Milo) dove into the bushes behind them and watched as the train rumbled by. Suddenly, the noise intensified. Stacy lowered her head to the ground and looked at the tracks. Behind the first train she could now see the shadow of a second train passing in the opposite direction.

"Another train!" Stacy shouted. "Southbound!"

Stacy sat up and peered through the bushes just in time to see the last of the passenger train cars go by, revealing the slow-moving southbound train behind it. The train was almost past them, though. Stacy could only count ten remaining cars.

"It's a freight train!" Stacy exclaimed, jumping to her feet. She looked to the wolves. "I know it's not the direction we wanted, but these trains probably only go by once a day. I think we should take it!"

There was no time to think it over. Wink took off running after the train and hopped into an open cargo car. Page, Tucker, Noah, Addison, and Everest followed behind him. Stacy grabbed Milo and stuffed him into her satchel and took off running. She pumped her arms as hard as she could, but her fastest wasn't fast enough. She looked up to see Everest leaning out of the car and reaching for her, but she couldn't get close enough to him. His silver eyes were wide with panic. *Oh no!* she thought, panting with effort. *What if I get left behind?*

Suddenly, Basil appeared beside her. Stacy hopped on

her back and Basil accelerated, running faster and faster until she was pacing the car that Everest and the others were in. Stacy reached for Everest and he pulled her into the train. Basil hopped in behind them.

The stars were just beginning to show up in the twilight sky as Stacy, the wolves, and Page wriggled up between the cars to the flat roof of the train. Everyone spread out and lay down to sleep, except for Everest, who positioned himself at the head of the train car to keep watch.

The steady motion of the train car was soothing.

Stacy reached her hand in her satchel to pet Milo. There was no turning back now. They were headed south and Stacy had no idea what biome she would wake up to. She leaned back against Wink and fell asleep.

ELEVEN

STACY OPENED HER eyes and then quickly closed them. *That can't be right.* Everything was orange. She opened them again and looked around in disbelief. It was as if the train they were on had transformed into a space shuttle during the night and flown them to another planet.

Stacy scanned the horizon for any trace of the familiar taiga, but they'd long left it behind. Everything around them—every rock, hill, and mountain—was a rusty shade of orange. *And the sky!* Juxtaposed against the coppery mountains, the sky was the most brilliant shade of blue Stacy had ever seen.

"A mesa biome!" Stacy whispered in wonder, sitting up.

All of the wolves and Page were already awake. Stacy opened the flap of her satchel, half expecting Milo to have flown back to the taiga during the night. Much to Stacy's surprise, the bat was still there. He opened one eye to the harsh mesa light and burrowed deeper inside. Stacy gave him a loving pat on the head and took out her binoculars so she could get a better view of the scenery.

Looking around, Stacy didn't know what to take in first. There were the large plateaus to the west of her, the tops of which were as flat as tables. Farther south was a cluster of tall, spindly rock formations Stacy knew were called hoodoos. And connecting everything, stretching as far as her eyes could see, was nothing but vast red sand and clay, punctuated by the occasional cactus and sagebrush.

"We should jump off here even though you all stick out like sore thumbs in this biome," Stacy said, looking at the white wolves and then over to her reddish dog. "You certainly blend in, Page. But look around—there's *no one* here to see any of you. There's no one here at all."

They waited until the train was passing a particularly cactus-free patch of the desert and then leapt into a soft red sand dune. Stacy looked around to make sure everyone was accounted for. They were all fine, except for Wink, who had managed to land on the one cactus in sight.

"Oh, Wink!" Stacy said, hurrying over to help him pick the needles out of his rear. Wink whined miserably.

After helping him pluck out most of the needles, Stacy and the group set off into the mesa. Stacy couldn't believe how beautiful the mesa biome was. Everywhere she looked she noticed something different—from the sprawling prickly pear cacti with hummingbirds flitting around them to the old Joshua trees with their spiky green leaves pointing skyward.

And the wildlife! Black-tailed jackrabbits raced from sagebrush to sagebrush while tiny baby quail scurried after their parents and massive golden eagles soared overhead.

"Noah, I don't think this biome suits you," Stacy teased as a sullen-looking Noah walked alongside her with his head down. "I haven't seen a single water source."

As soon as the words left Stacy's lips, she realized this was a much bigger issue than she had initially thought.

What she had meant to be a silly joke to Noah was actually a very real threat. *Where are we going to find water?* Stacy's wolves drank quite a bit of water each day, and the canteens she had brought from the taiga were nearly empty. As soon as she thought about it, Stacy began to feel thirsty.

"All right, everyone," Stacy said. "Here's the plan. We're looking for somewhere we can set up camp for a couple of months, but it needs to have a water source."

Stacy reached into her satchel and pulled out a groggy Milo. She gently tossed him into the air and he started happily fluttering about, looking like he was glad to stretch his wings at last.

"Milo here can keep us aware of any mesa animals that might be in need of our rescue services," Stacy said.

Basil scrambled up some jagged rocks and looked around, her head held high as she tried to spot something new in the unfamiliar landscape.

"Anything, girl?" Stacy asked.

Basil nodded, so Stacy and the others made their way up the rocks as well, until they could see what Basil was looking at. In the distance, probably about a mile from where they were standing, was a tiny village made up of two rows of dilapidated wooden buildings that looked like they hadn't been lived in for years.

"I know what that is," Stacy said, jumping off the rock pile and heading toward the village.

"That's a ghost town."

TWELVE

THE DESERTED TOWN seemed strangely silent—quieter, somehow, than the rest of the mesa around it. Several of the ramshackle wooden buildings had lost their windows and red sand had blown across the floors, piling into little dunes in the corners. There was what looked like an abandoned church on one end of the row of buildings, and a blacksmith on the other, its sign weather-beaten but still legible. A wooden water tower loomed over the rest of the town, leaning to one side as if it might fall at any moment. One building looked like it might have been a saloon; another an old bank.

Stacy pressed her face against a dirty window that

still remained in one of the buildings and saw rows of old-fashioned desks inside. *It must have been a school-house.*

She was tempted to go inside, although it looked completely bare except for the desks; maybe there were old books stashed somewhere. But when she looked at her wolves, she lost interest in exploring. They were all panting. Wink flopped down in the shade of the school-house, looking hot and miserable. She had to find them water. Soon.

"You don't suppose . . ." Stacy said, reaching into Noah's pack and pulling out a canteen while looking up at the rickety water tower.

Noah eagerly ran over to the rusty pump that fed into a barrel at its base and pumped it several times. The pump hissed and sizzled and then spurted out a short blast of brown water before weakening to just a drip.

"Well, it was worth a try, Noah," Stacy said, screwing the cap back on her canteen. "Let's go, everyone."

Stacy and the pack continued walking west from the ghost town through the desert, following the setting sun.

"Wow," Stacy said, looking at the horizon. "I think sunsets in the mesa are one of the most beautiful things I've ever seen."

They wandered a bit longer. Stacy noticed everyone

was yawning, herself included. She knew her wolves needed some type of liquid. Suddenly, she had an idea of how to get them rehydrated.

"Let's set up temporary camp for the night before it gets too much darker," she said to the group. "Here is just as good a place as any."

The wolves circled back to where Stacy was standing and began prepping for the long night ahead of them. Basil and Noah started collecting rocks and positioning them in a circle so Stacy could build a fire. Everest was sniffing the area thoroughly, always on the lookout for potential danger. Tucker curled up with Page and Milo and began grooming them, while Wink continued to pick the last of the cactus needles out of his rump with his teeth.

"Addi, could you give me a hand?" Stacy called out to Addison. The amber-eyed wolf came over to where Stacy was standing in front of a towering prickly pear cactus. "Here, hold this, please."

Stacy hung her leather satchel around Addison's neck with the flap flipped open. Next, she took her hunting knife and began chopping the purple fruit off the top of the cactus cladodes. Once there were twenty or so of the fruit on the ground, Stacy carefully used her knife to spear them. Then she used a stick to knock them from the tip of her knife into the satchel Addison was holding.

When the satchel was full of fruit, Stacy and Addison went over to the circle of stones, where Basil and Noah had placed a pile of kindling. Examining the wood more closely, Stacy saw that the wolves had gathered dried sagebrush branches. *Those'll probably smell good when they burn,* she thought. There was even a small heap of additional branches outside the stone circle, so that they could keep the fire burning for as long as they needed.

Taking out the flint and steel Basil had given her, Stacy rested the end of the C-shaped steel near the pile of kindling and scraped it quickly with the flint. There was no spark. Stacy tried again, and again. *This should be easier for me than for Basil,* she thought, frustrated. *I have hands, after all!*

Basil nudged the flint with her nose, changing the angle slightly, then nodded to Stacy. Gritting her teeth, Stacy tried again.

This time, a bright spark flew off the flint and onto the kindling. Dropping onto her belly, Stacy blew gently on the spark, coaxing it into a flame. Basil panted approvingly.

Once the fire was burning brightly, Stacy turned to Addison and took the satchel from her, pouring the prickly pears out onto the ground.

"Careful," she told the wolves, who were looking at them curiously. "Those thorns are sharp!" The egg-shaped purple fruits were covered with dozens of tiny hairlike thorns. She had to be careful not to touch the skin of the pear, or the thorns would embed themselves into her hands. Stacy grabbed a pointy sage branch from the pile and speared one of the pears with it. She held it over the fire until the thorns had been singed off. After letting it cool, she picked up her old hunting knife and cut into the fruit, making a deep slit in its skin. Inside, she could see the dark purple fruit, studded with tiny seeds.

Stacy chopped it into several pieces. "Try this," she said to Addison and Basil.

The female wolves nosed the fruit warily. They had gotten used to eating pumpkin and sometimes apples or berries, but prickly pear was far from an Arctic wolf's natural diet.

Stacy picked up a piece of the pulpy fruit and popped it into her own mouth. "Oh!" she gasped in delight. The watery juice flooded her dry mouth, beginning to quench her thirst. "It's as good as a drink," she explained. Basil and Addison, encouraged, each took a bite.

Stacy peeled pears until she, Page, and the wolves weren't thirsty anymore. They also shared a couple of loaves of bread and some dried berries, almost the last of what she had brought from their pantry back at the cave. She offered a pear to Milo, but he seemed happy to flap through the air, hunting insects.

By the time the moon was high in the sky, everyone had had enough to eat. *We'll have to find new food sources soon,* Stacy thought. The mesa had gotten chillier after the sun set, and she was glad they had the crackling fire to keep them warm. She and Page and the wolves curled up together as they always did. Tonight, Stacy rested her head on Tucker's back and gazed up at the glittering stars. She pulled her necklace from beneath her striped shirt and looked at the charms as they reflected the starlight. *My human parents gave these to me,* she thought. For a moment, it felt as if they were with her and her pack.

Just as Stacy was drifting off to sleep, a loud coyote howl rang out over the mesa.

THIRTEEN

WITHIN SECONDS, AN entire cacophony of coyote howls could be heard, first coming from the north. And then, a minute later, another pack replying from the south. Stacy and her pack were caught in the middle.

"What do we do?" Stacy whispered, straining to see any of her wolves' faces with the low light from the embers that were left of their campfire. Everest opened one eye and twitched an ear at her. Tucker yawned.

Stacy realized the wolves were unfazed by the coyotes. *Interesting,* she thought. While the idea of dozens of scrappy coyotes was terrifying to her, Stacy's wolves knew their place at the top of the food chain and were completely unworried. She instantly felt safer and nestled in closer to Page and Tucker. Finally, she drifted off to sleep, the coyote howls echoing in her ears.

The next morning, the group set off in search of a better campsite. Somewhere a little less out in the open and with a water source, and (if Stacy had her way) not in the middle of rival coyote packs.

They headed south toward the hoodoos, much to Stacy's delight. She'd read a page about them in an H encyclopedia book she had. She had pored over the pages for honeybees, hoodoos, horses, horticulture, and hot springs. And lamented that she didn't have books for more of the letters of the alphabet. Stacy had been especially fascinated by the hoodoos—how majestic they were . . . how each one was unique, kind of like the mesa's fingerprints . . . how they were actually formed by water, but now resided in dry desert biomes. She was quite excited to see one in person.

As they approached the hoodoos, Stacy hopped onto Wink's back so she could stare up at them without tripping. She couldn't get over how tall they were. And up close she could see that they almost appeared to be striped, with different-colored striations in the rocks.

Suddenly there was a bat blocking her view.

"Milo, move," Stacy said, swatting the air gently, not

to actually hit Milo but to get her point across that he was blocking her breathtaking view of the hoodoos.

But Milo was relentless. He circled around Stacy's head and then flew over to Page, whose ears were swiveling wildly.

"Wait, a rescue?" Stacy asked. She knew Milo could alert them to an animal rescue at any time, but for some reason Stacy had assumed it would be after they had settled into their mesa home and built a proper campsite. But an animal in trouble had to be their priority.

"All right, Milo," Stacy said. "Lead the way!"

The wolves and Page raced down the steep trails surrounding the hoodoos with Stacy still on Wink's back. Stacy was relieved she wasn't running herself when she looked over the side of the switchbacks they were traversing and saw the small rocks rolling straight down the sides of the thin trail they were on.

Milo came to an abrupt stop in the middle of the trail, causing all the wolves to dig their paws into the red dirt, sending more rocks and pebbles careening off the trail and into the ravines on either side of them. Stacy's eyes followed the falling rocks as they rolled down and down until they landed about twenty feet below her at the bottom of the ravine next to a small donkey. *A donkey!*

The donkey was gray with patches of white on his ears and his muzzle. He had a saddle, a saddlebag, and a striped blanket draped over his back. He didn't appear injured, but he looked sad. Stacy couldn't tell if he looked so sad because that's how all donkeys looked, or if it was because he was at the bottom of a ravine.

"He's stuck," Stacy said. "It's too steep for him to climb up."

Stacy hopped off Wink and, before she could form a plan with the wolves, she was sliding (or falling, rather) down the red sand on the side of the ravine. She landed with a soft thud next to the donkey.

"Oops!" Stacy said, hopping up and steadying herself by placing her hands on the donkey's back. "Well, I can see how you could have slid down here accidentally. I'm just going to climb back up and talk to my wolf pack about how best to rescue you. Don't worry, they aren't interested in eating you. We do this kind of thing all the time. Animal rescues, that is, not finding donkeys in ravines next to hoodoos. No, that's definitely a first." The donkey nosed curiously at her face, and Stacy patted him on his muzzle. "I'm rambling. You don't understand me. I'm going to gooooo . . . but I'll be right back."

Stacy started to walk up the side of the ravine, but

slid right back down to where she started with every step she took.

Okay, this should make for an interesting animal rescue. It appears that I need rescuing now, too. Stacy peered up at her wolves and Page, who were all staring down at her with concerned expressions.

"Not to worry, guys!" Stacy hollered up to them. "I came down to, uh, assess the situation. Noah, could you please throw me that rope from your pack?"

Noah reached into the pack, pulled out the rope with his teeth, and tossed it down to where Stacy and the donkey were standing, keeping one end of it in his mouth.

"Great!" Stacy shouted. "Okay, now I'm going to need a bunch of small, sturdy sticks, about three feet in length. I think I saw some dead bushes a little ways back on the trail that you might be able to break."

The wolves and Page disappeared for a few minutes. One by one they returned with sticks in their mouths that they then tossed down to Stacy. While they continued tossing down the sticks, Stacy rummaged through the donkey's saddlebag for anything that might prove useful to their current situation. There wasn't much, but there was rope—good, sturdy climbing rope—and that was all that Stacy needed to begin to formulate an escape plan.

She took one of the sticks and lashed it onto the climbing rope so that a piece of the stick poked out from either side of the rope. She repeated this, spacing the sticks about two feet apart, until she'd reached the end of the rope. Then, she tied off a large loop at one of the ends and tossed it up the hill, where Everest caught it.

"All right," she muttered to herself. "Time to see if this works."

Leaning forward onto the slope of the ravine, Stacy grabbed hold of the highest stick she could reach on the rope. She held the stick with both hands on opposite sides of the rope and then did the same with her feet, stepping up onto the stick closest to her boots. She wobbled back and forth for a bit, but it worked—the stick that her feet were on sank into the sand, giving her a sturdy foothold that prevented her from sliding back down. The line of sticks would form a track to support her feet as she walked.

"Okay," Stacy said. "It works for me. Whether I can teach a donkey to do it is another matter entirely."

Stacy looked up at Everest. He was holding the rope in his mouth and suddenly realized what Stacy was about to do. He quickly motioned for all the other wolves to grab hold of the rope. Meanwhile, Noah tightened his hold on the vine rope that Stacy was grasping as a guide.

"Okay, here goes nothing," Stacy said, hopping onto the donkey and holding the vine rope in one hand while taking the reins in her other. The donkey brayed loudly and then took a step forward.

"Easy," Stacy said softly. "Easy, boy."

Stacy had never used reins before. She'd never ridden a horse before, let alone a donkey. But she realized she was going to need to learn how to use reins pretty quickly if she had any hope of getting this donkey out of the ravine.

Luckily, the donkey had naturally found the first stick on his own when he'd stepped forward. Now, the tricky part would be getting him to take the perfect step forward to the next one, in hopes he would find his footing again. If Stacy could get him to do that, she was pretty confident she could guide him in a straight line up and out of the ravine. But if he didn't step in the right places, the track of sticks in the sand wouldn't stop his hooves from sliding backward.

Stacy and the donkey walked back and forth for what must have been half an hour. Stacy imagined they must have looked as if they were dancing. It was midday now and the sun was directly over Stacy's head, beating down on her and the donkey. She was covered in sweat, but determined to succeed in this rescue.

All of a sudden, Stacy saw Wink flying through the air above her. He jumped the full twenty feet down the ravine and landed, surprisingly gracefully, at Stacy's feet.

"Wink!" Stacy exclaimed. She stared at his legs, which were firmly planted in the red sand. "How did you do that and not break every bone in your body?" Wink shrugged and positioned himself behind the donkey. The donkey snorted and jerked his head up and down. He definitely did not like being this close to a wolf. Quickly, he stepped forward and started walking up the track of sticks in the sand, with Wink guiding his hooves toward each stick, one after the other.

"Good job!" Stacy shouted, looking over her shoulder at Wink, whose nose was just inches from the donkey's behind. "Don't let him take any steps backward!"

The donkey had figured out how to step on the sunken footholds by this point, and took off up the ravine, trying to get away from Wink. As soon as he reached the top, though, he saw there were five wolves waiting for him, and he reared back on his hind legs, braying with fear.

Stacy almost toppled backward. For a moment, she hung dizzyingly over the edge of the ravine. She quickly swung her leg over the donkey's back and managed to jump off. She scrambled up the rest of the rope ladder, pulling on the reins so hard that the donkey had no choice but to come down from his hind legs and walk the rest of the way up the ravine and onto the trail, resisting all the way.

"Back up, guys," Stacy said to her wolves. "Give him some space. We don't want him falling down again."

The wolves retreated about ten yards down the trail, including an exhausted Wink, while Stacy looked over the donkey one last time to make sure he didn't have any injuries.

"You probably travel this trail every day, huh, boy," Stacy said to him, untying the sticks and stuffing the climbing rope into her satchel and pulling out an apple and feeding it to the donkey. "Go on then, and catch up with your group. Hopefully they won't miss this rope too much."

The donkey ate the apple and buried his muzzle into the crook of Stacy's arm. She pressed her face against his.

"Everest, can donkeys live in the taiga?" Stacy yelled back to the pack's alpha. She knew the answer, though. The big white alpha shook his head no.

"I'm going to miss you, boy," she whispered to the donkey. "Be good."

And with that, the donkey let out a happy bray and

began lumbering down the switchbacks in search of his own pack.

"That donkey obviously belonged to someone," Stacy said to her wolves as they returned to where she stood. "Either tourists or tour guides . . . I'd like to avoid both if possible, so I think we should head back north to camp."

The group retraced their steps from the morning, passing their campsite from the previous night and heading into the low mountains to the north. This was exactly the type of rugged terrain Stacy had been hoping to find when she first hatched her plan to hide out away from the taiga for a month or two. The chance that another person would be out here in the desert mesas was very slim.

They were just coming up to a flat stretch of trail when Stacy looked up from the steep pathway she was navigating and let out a sharp gasp that sounded a lot like a horse neighing. She was right about not seeing another person, but she had completely forgotten about mountain lions.

And there was one standing right in front of her.

FOURTEEN

THE MOUNTAIN LION was crouched on a boulder a little above the trail, her pale gold eyes trained intently on Stacy. Everest pushed protectively in front of her and Page, fur bristling along his spine. The lion's ears flattened slightly, her muscles tensing, and her long tail switched from side to side. She looked ready to leap.

Mountain lions don't usually attack people, Stacy reminded herself, remembering a book on wildlife she had read back in the taiga. *And she certainly won't attack the wolves. Not unless she's frightened and doesn't see another way out.*

The only one of her pack really in danger was Page.

As if she'd come to the same conclusion, Page pressed against Stacy's leg, whimpering slightly. Basil stepped forward beside Everest, blocking the little dog from the mountain lion's view. Everest growled at the mountain lion and tensed, preparing to lunge.

Somebody's going to get hurt.

"Stop!" Stacy said urgently, wrapping an arm around Everest's neck and pulling him backward. "This is *her* home."

The huge alpha gave her a look of annoyance, but slightly relaxed his tense stance, no longer poised to attack. Careful not to turn her back on the mountain lion, Stacy let go of Everest and glanced out the corner of her eye at the rest of the pack. Noah and Tucker were poised to back up Basil and Everest if a fight broke out, while Addison was looking thoughtful. Wink stood protectively beside Page, his usually playful expression now serious.

"Everyone calm down," Stacy said. She tried to remember what the book said to do when you encounter a mountain lion. *Try to look big,* it had said. *Maintain eye contact. Don't turn your back on them. And whatever you do, don't run.*

Stacy raised her arms above her head, spreading them wide. "Back away," she told her pack. "We're not going to attack her in her own territory. She belongs here. We're just visiting." She kept her own emerald eyes on the golden gaze of the lion and took a step backward. "It's okay," she said in a calm voice. "We're not here to fight you. We're leaving."

Stacy backed away a little farther. "Come on, guys," she said. Reluctantly, the wolves shuffled backward.

With a final long look at them, the mountain lion turned, slipped quietly down from the boulder, and disappeared from sight among the red rocks and scrubby thornbushes of the slope. Stacy let out a relieved breath and lowered her arms.

"I think we should follow a different trail," she told the others. Everest huffed in agreement.

Scrambling back down the steep pathway, one hand on Addison's back for balance, Stacy kept a sharp eye out for other animals.

As they found another trail that wound high into the mountains, Stacy could tell the rest of her pack was keeping watch as well. Basil kept dashing ahead to scout the territory, her fur flashing white through the underbrush as she made wide circles and then returned. Everest, Tucker, and Addison paused frequently to scent the air and look around suspiciously. And Wink stuck close to Page's side, guarding his small friend.

When Noah stopped dead in his tracks, pricked up his ears, and sniffed the air, Stacy thought he was checking for another mountain lion. But then the blue-eyed wolf shot off the trail as if he'd been launched out of a cannon, scrambling up the steep side of the mesa. The rest of the pack watched, heads jerking up in surprise, then started to follow him, one by one.

Stacy grabbed hold of the thick fur between Tucker's shoulders to help herself up the slope. After a few steps, she heard a whine behind her. Stacy turned and saw Page trying to scramble after them. Wink was below Page, trying to help by nudging her forward. The mountainside was too steep for the little dog.

How could she carry Page and climb at the same time? Page was just a little too big to fit into Stacy's satchel with the supplies already in there. While Stacy hesitated, Wink lay down on his belly and Page climbed onto his back, taking hold of the tuft of fur at the back of his neck with her teeth.

"Good thinking, Wink," Stacy said. "Can you hang on, Page?" Both Wink and Page wagged their tails.

As they climbed the slope, Page, Addison, and Wink all kept sniffing the air, their eyes bright with excitement, their ears perked up. It was clear that all three of them could hear and smell something Stacy couldn't.

But after what seemed like an endless time of hot, exhausting climbing, she finally heard it.

Running water. It was just a trickle, not a rushing river, but there was definitely water somewhere up ahead.

The sound gave Stacy new energy. The prickly pear fruit had helped to quench their thirst, but the thought of actual water was *amazing*.

When she and Addison, followed by Wink with Page on his back, finally scrambled up to the ledge on the top of the cliff, at first they didn't see the rest of the pack. Instead, there was the flat ledge and, on the cliff face, a dark square opening, supported by heavy timbers.

Stacy looked at it dubiously. "It's definitely man-made," she said. "It looks a little like the iron mine back in the taiga. You don't think . . ."

The sound of water was coming from inside. Cautiously, Stacy walked forward to peer in, Addison and Wink on either side of her, Page still riding proudly on Wink's back.

Inside, the square entrance opened into a wide cave. Stacy stepped inside. It was dark and refreshingly cool after the heat of the mesa. Taking a deep breath, she let the cold soak into her skin and begin to cool her down. She could hear splashing and saw a flash of white fur. Something glittered in the rock wall.

As her eyes adjusted, Stacy realized that she couldn't see the back of the cave. It seemed to go on and on, disappearing into darkness like a vast tunnel. She could see the marks of picks on the walls. There was a broken-down old cart close to the entrance, and a pile of objects near it. Examining the pile, Stacy saw a couple of picks and hammers with worn wooden handles, and a ragged old sack.

It's an abandoned gold mine, Stacy realized. The cave really *was* the entrance to a huge tunnel, which must go on and on and down into the heart of the mesa.

Addison's cool nose touched Stacy's hand, calling her attention back to the cave. There was a happy yelp— *Basil,* she thought—and splashing over to her right. Wink and Page hurried past her, eager to join the fun. She and Addison followed.

Near the side of the tunnel, a spring bubbled up from the ground, and ran down the rock deeper into the cave. Noah was lying happily in the middle of the spring, water flowing over him, plastering his fur to his sides. Everest stood beside him, his big paws sunk into the water and an expression of pure happiness on his face. Page, Tucker, Basil, and Wink had their noses in the water and Addison joined them, dipping her face down to take a long drink.

Fresh water! Now that she saw it, Stacy was suddenly thirstier than she had ever been. She waded into the spring, which came up only a few inches above her ankles, and bent down, cupping her hands to scoop up water. She drank in long, deep gulps, the cold water running down her throat. Water streamed over her feet, cooling and refreshing her, and she drank and drank.

When she finally wasn't thirsty anymore, Stacy waded back out of the spring to investigate the mine. Page followed her, shaking her thick coat vigorously as soon as she was out and splattering Stacy with more water. Everest came, too, his heavy fur dripping.

Stacy couldn't tell how far back or how deep into the mountain the mine went. A few steps past where the rest of the wolves were still playing in the water, it became too dark to see. "Hello, hello," she called, and her voice echoed back as though the mineshaft went on a very long way. Milo took off into the darkness of the mineshaft.

"You don't think there's anything else alive in here, do you?" she asked, and Everest snorted and shook his head. "No, I'm sure you checked." Before he drank, Everest would have scented the cave carefully to make sure no other animals were living there. Retreating a little from the darkness of the mineshaft, Stacy looked around the mine entrance again.

It was a wide cave with a level floor. The spring ran along one side, but the rest of the mine entrance seemed pretty dry. It was pleasantly cool after the heat of the mesa, but not too cold. Light came in from the entrance. *We'd be sheltered in here,* Stacy thought, looking up at the cave roof, *and we could even build a fire on the ledge right outside.*

This was much better than where they'd made camp the night before.

"Are you thinking what I'm thinking?" she asked Everest. The silver-eyed alpha looked slowly around the mine entrance and back up at her. Then, deliberately, he lay down on the cave floor and sprawled out, looking totally relaxed. Page yipped and licked his ear.

"That's right," Stacy said, and sat down beside him. The stones were smooth and cool beneath her. "Home sweet home . . . until we can go back to the taiga."

FIFTEEN

SUNSHINE STREAMING THROUGH the mine entrance woke Stacy early the next morning. The cave was cool, but she was warm and cozy, nestled in the middle of the heap of wolves, Page curled beside her hip. Stacy was cuddled up to Tucker, her head on Everest's side and her back against Addison.

Carefully, Stacy got up, trying not to wake anyone else. As soon as she was on her feet, Page jumped up and looked at her expectantly. Everest lifted his head and yawned. Addison opened one eye, and Wink rolled onto his back and gazed at her, his paws sticking straight up in the air. Tucker and Noah didn't move, but Stacy was pretty sure they had woken, too.

"Okay, okay," she said, laughing. "I'm not that stealthy."

She went over to the spring, took a drink, and washed her face. Behind her, she could hear the wolves getting to their feet, stretching and yawning. Stacy dug in her satchel, pulling out a peeled prickly pear and the last loaf of bread. Now there was nothing but a few pieces of fruit left. Stacy divided the bread with Page, who sniffed it doubtfully, but ate it.

"Do you want some?" Stacy asked, offering the bread to the wolves. None of them stepped forward, and Everest huffed through his nose, indicating that Stacy should eat it herself.

We need to get more food, Stacy worried.

In the wild, wolves often ate only one big meal every week or so. Back in the taiga, her wolves had gotten used to eating with Stacy every day, but they would be fine for several more days without eating. Stacy and Page, though, needed to eat more often.

The pack didn't hunt in the taiga, because there they rescued the woodland creatures that were their natural prey. Without a river where Noah could fish or some other type of food source, though, she was pretty sure the wolves would hunt the animals of the desert biome rather than let Stacy and Page go hungry.

But she really didn't want it to come to that.

Stacy knew there had to be a river nearby somewhere. It was just a matter of locating it. With a fresh day in front of her, she figured she'd let some of the wolves rest in the mineshaft while she and Everest explored their new surroundings. But just as Stacy was fastening her satchel, she heard flapping wings.

"Milo!" Stacy exclaimed, happy that the bat had found them again.

Milo swooped through the air around Stacy and then fluttered excitedly around Page's head. The little dog, her big ears held high, yapped questioningly at him and then looked up at Stacy.

"Another rescue?" Stacy asked. "I guess you've made quick work of getting to know the local bats. Okay, Milo, lead the way." She, Page, and the wolves hurried after him out of the mine.

Outside, Milo flew over the entrance to the mine and above the top of the mesa. Stacy and the rest of the pack scrambled after him. Above the mine, the mesa flattened into a plateau, and Stacy and the wolves were able to move quickly.

Stacy didn't see the canyon until she was right on top of it. Skidding to a stop, her boots at the canyon's edge, Stacy teetered dizzyingly for a moment. Then a firm tug yanked her backward. Taking a deep relieved breath, Stacy turned to see that Everest had grabbed on to the back of her shirt with his teeth.

"Thanks, Everest," she said gratefully.

Milo dipped down into the canyon. Stacy watched him fly lower and lower. It was a slot canyon, she realized, a split in the mesa much deeper than it was wide. The two sides of the canyon were striated with different layers of red, yellow, and tan rock and honeycombed with cracks and ridges. In some places, the sides of the canyon almost touched, and it looked like they were less than six feet apart most of the way down. But it was a very long way to the bottom.

Milo was hovering over a ledge about halfway down the side of the canyon. Stacy leaned forward to see more clearly. She couldn't believe what she was looking at.

"Oh, no!" There was a small black, brown, and white dog huddled on a narrow ledge below them. Its long ears were drooping, and it looked very scared.

"Looks like some kind of beagle mix," Stacy said. "How on earth did a dog wind up all the way out here?"

The top of the canyon was ridged and sloping enough that the dog probably could have scrambled along it pretty easily, but then there was a long drop to the ledge it was resting on. There was no way the dog could climb up or down.

"I wonder how long it has been down there," Stacy said. Tucker, the healer of the pack, whined apprehensively. The sun was very hot, but nights spent on the exposed rock of the canyon must be cold. And there was no food or water.

"We have to get it out of there as soon as possible," Stacy said. *But how?*

If they walked a bit away from where the little dog was trapped, they could then start to scramble partway down the canyon walls leading up to where the dog had gotten stuck, she thought. And, if she braced herself *between* the walls of the canyon where they were at their closest, Stacy might be able to get far enough down to drop onto the narrow ledge beside the dog. Only Stacy would be able to do that, however—wolf bodies weren't built that way.

It was a *very* narrow ledge, with a long fall beneath it. Stacy would have to be careful to drop in the exact right place so that she didn't either land on the dog or miss the ledge completely.

Cautiously, Stacy started to move toward the cliff edge. Everest growled and took hold of her sleeve in his mouth, pulling her to a halt again.

"I'm not going to jump in," Stacy told him, but the wolf's eyes narrowed and he yanked on her sleeve. Stacy stopped and looked down at Everest. "We'll do it together," she promised, "and we'll be safe. I just have to figure out how."

Everest held her sleeve tightly between his teeth for a moment longer and then let go. Stacy opened her satchel and dug out the long rope of knotted vines. "It's not long enough to connect all of us," she said, "but if Everest, Noah, Tucker, and I go, we can tie it between us so that if one of us falls the others will pull us back up."

There was another step to her plan, but she didn't want to tell Everest about it until they'd already completed the first stage of the rescue.

Basil growled. Wink and Addison looked disapproving: they did *not* want to be left behind. And Stacy was sure Addison had figured out that this wasn't Stacy's whole plan—she must see that the four of them roped together wouldn't be able to make it all the way down to the little dog.

Stacy knelt down beside them. "I need you to be up here so you can move quickly if someone needs help," she told Basil. "And I need you to look after Page and make sure she doesn't try to follow us," she said, turning to Wink. Taking a deep breath, she looked into Addison's eyes. "I need *you* to trust me, Addi," she said, taking off her satchel and hanging it around Addison's neck. Addison looked back at Stacy and, after a moment, blinked slowly in agreement.

As the other wolves watched and Page paced anxiously between them, Stacy and the others walked several hundred feet back along the slot canyon opening. Next, she tied herself, Tucker, Everest, and Noah together, wrapping the vine around her own waist and behind the wolves' shoulders. "It's a good thing I practiced tying knots so much," she said finally, tugging at the rope. "I think these will hold." She looked back at the wolves who were staying behind. "If anything happens, we'll see you back at the mine," she shouted firmly. "Do *not* try to come down after us."

Stacy began her descent, Everest behind her, followed by Tucker, and finally Noah. At first, the slope of the canyon was gentle enough that they could all walk along its ridges, scrambling from one ridge to the next. Soon, Stacy was on her hands and knees, gripping the rock for balance.

But they were only about a third of the way down the canyon when they reached the last walkable ridge. Below that, the slope fell, steep and smooth, down about thirty feet to where the little dog lay. It was obvious she was going to need to jump.

That's a long drop, Stacy worried, looking down at the dog. *What if it has broken bones? I need to hurry.*

Tucker and Noah were looking up at Stacy, confused, but Everest huffed, outraged. "I'm sorry," Stacy told him sincerely. "But you would have tried to stop me from going. Now we're so close, you're going to listen to my plan." Everest growled and shook his head, baring his teeth angrily.

"Look at it," Stacy said, gesturing down at the dog. "It *needs* us. Its owners obviously abandoned it. We're the only ones who can help." Everest glanced down at the small huddled figure on the ridge below, and Stacy saw his eyes soften. "I can do it," she said quickly. "And I'll be safe."

Stacy freed herself from the vine rope that had kept her and the wolves together. She reached into Noah's pack and pulled out the climbing rope from the donkey rescue.

She reached behind her back to the bow that Tucker had given her for her rescue day, and one of the arrows. She took the climbing rope and tied it to the arrow, tying the other end of the rope around her waist. "I've been practicing," she said, notching the arrow. Taking aim on a long, deep-looking crack on the opposite wall of the canyon, Stacy fired the arrow.

The arrow hit the canyon wall a little below the crack, bounced off, and fell. "I should have practiced *more*," Stacy muttered, and used the rope to pull it back toward her.

It took five tries, but at last the arrow shot straight into the crack and disappeared. Stacy yanked on the rope, but the arrow held fast—she hoped it was wedged firmly into the thinnest part of the crack.

"See, the rope will hold my weight if I fall," Stacy explained to the wolves, pulling hard on it. "Which I *won't*. And the rope is long enough that once I get the dog I can rappel the rest of the way down to the canyon floor."

Everest growled, his jaw tightly clenched. Noah whined. Tucker stared at her in distress. Stacy walked to where the opposite wall of the canyon was closest and sat on the very edge of the ridge. She could just touch the other wall with her feet. Looking down, she could see that it narrowed a little farther below her. She wrapped the excess rope around her waist several times and then several times around her wrists. Gritting her teeth, she pushed off the ridge and, hanging on to the rope, let herself fall.

She fell about ten feet before, with a jolt, she managed to grab on to a large rock and stop herself, right above where the canyon narrowed enough for her to brace her back and her feet on its opposite walls. Stacy took a deep breath and, keeping her body stiff, slowly began to move her feet down, one after the other, her back scraping against the canyon wall.

It seemed to take hours to slowly rappel her way down

to the narrow ridge where the little dog lay. Clouds had covered the sun, so it wasn't blinding her, and she could see the worried faces of Everest, Tucker, and Noah peering down at her.

Finally, Stacy's feet felt the ledge the dog was on. She dropped down the last little bit, landing ungracefully on her knees. She felt like she'd been scraped raw, but she quickly got to her feet, looking for the little dog.

The long-eared dog, a girl, was lying on the ledge, but she looked up at Stacy with big brown eyes and gave a soft whine.

"You poor thing," Stacy said. She knelt beside the dog and ran her hands over her soft fur, feeling for broken bones. There didn't seem to be any, and the dog didn't flinch from her hands as if she was in pain, but she felt very thin. Stacy stroked her back. "I'm going to help you," she said. "Don't be scared." A raindrop hit her arm, then another.

"We'd better get off this ledge," Stacy told the dog. Looking up at the wolves, she called, "She's all right!"

Stacy untied the rope from around her waist and dropped it down from the ledge. It dangled about five feet off the canyon floor. "Perfect," she said to herself.

It was beginning to rain hard. Stacy wiped the rain from her eyes and knelt down to pick up the little dog.

She hesitated. A trickling echoed through the canyon behind her, growing louder and louder, until it was a rushing, deafening noise. *What in the world?*

Suddenly, Stacy jerked her head up, terrified. *A flash flood!*

SIXTEEN

STACY LOOKED UP at the wall of water as it barreled down the slot canyon toward her. It reached Noah, Everest, and Tucker first, knocking them off their feet. Stacy braced herself for the water to crash down on her, curling protectively around the little dog. Suddenly, out of nowhere, Basil appeared alongside her, ricocheting at lightning speed along the walls of the canyon. She grabbed the little dog out of Stacy's arms by the scruff of her neck and continued racing down the gorge. It happened in less than a second. Stacy took a deep breath, filling her lungs with as much oxygen as she could. And then the water slammed into her.

Swept along by the rushing torrent, Stacy struggled to keep her head above water. The water surged forward. Stacy took one deep breath, and then she was sucked under.

Stacy tumbled over and over, losing track of which direction was the surface. Her arm scraped stingingly along the side of the canyon.

Stacy's chest felt like it was burning. She needed to breathe, soon. Black spots swam in front of her eyes. *I have to stay awake,* she thought desperately. *I have to get to high ground.*

There was a firm tug on the back of her shirt. Stacy struggled for a second—was she caught on something?—but then realized she was being pulled purposefully along. Her head broke through the surface of the water. Stacy pulled in a long breath of air and coughed.

Twisting her head around, she looked back to see who was pulling her through the water. Intense blue eyes stared back at her from Noah's furry face, his jaw locked onto the back of her shirt.

"Noah," Stacy said. "Thank you for saving me! Is everyone else okay?"

Noah grunted, tugging Stacy toward the edge of the rapidly moving water. It was shallower here, Stacy realized, as if the flash flood was already exhausting

its energy. The rain had stopped. Looking around, she saw that they had been washed out of the canyon—the slopes on either side of the riverbed were shallow. Probably this was a channel that water from earlier floods had made as it rushed out of the canyon.

Everest and Tucker were already on the muddy riverbank, along with Stacy's bow and arrow that had washed up on the shore. Tucker was collapsed on the ground, panting hard. Everest was pacing back and forth, his eyes scanning the water. When he caught sight of Stacy, he hurried forward and took hold of her shoulder firmly with his huge jaw, helping Noah bring her in to land. Tucker got to his paws and hurried over to nose along Stacy's body, checking her for injuries. He licked her arm, which she realized now was scraped and bleeding. Her arm instantly felt better as Tucker tended to it.

All three wolves were soaked, their thick white pelts plastered close to their bodies. Noah shook himself hard, water droplets flying everywhere.

"Noah!" Stacy said. "I'm wet enough already." He grinned at her, his tongue lolling out as if he was laughing. Basil was nearby with the little dog. Stacy and the others ran over to them.

"Basil, you were incredible," Stacy said, beaming.

"Did you know you could do that?" Basil shook her head no. It was clear she was very winded. After checking the little dog for injuries, Tucker began to vigorously lick her fur the wrong way—Stacy knew that this would help her dry off faster.

Stacy felt warm and content watching them. They were so lucky that all six of them had survived the flash flood without serious injuries. *All thanks to Noah and Basil,* she thought. She ran her fingers through her sopping-wet hair and then felt around her face and neck for any cuts or scrapes. She gasped, suddenly realizing what was missing. "My necklace!"

The wolves looked up at her, their faces worried.

"I was wearing the charms from the bracelet Everest gave me," Stacy explained, staring down at her empty neck. "It must have slipped off when I was underwater." Hot tears filled her eyes. Those charms had been the only thing she had from the human family she didn't remember. Now they were gone, too.

Everest pressed his muzzle against her hand and whined sympathetically. "Thanks, Everest," Stacy said softly, twining her fingers in his thick white fur. Losing the necklace hurt, but it helped to know that her new family—her pack—was there for her.

Noah strode decisively toward the rushing floodwaters. With a shock, Stacy suddenly realized what he was planning to do.

"Noah!" she shouted. "No!" She ran toward him, but she was too late. Noah dove smoothly into the water, disappearing from sight.

Stacy and Everest raced to the water's edge. She began to count the seconds Noah was underwater. When she got to twenty, fear took over and she began to shake. *Where is he?* Stacy strained her eyes, trying to catch sight of white fur in the turbulent water. But there was nothing. Stacy bent her knees, preparing to dive into the water. It didn't matter that the flood had almost swept her away; she couldn't let Noah drown without trying to save him.

A tug on her wrist pulled her backward. Everest was gripping her wrist gently between his teeth. She tried to pull away, but he clamped down more firmly, narrowing his eyes at her.

"We have to help him!" Stacy said. Tears were running down her cheeks now, but she kept trying to reach the water. She didn't know how she was going to save Noah—he was a much stronger swimmer than she was—but she had to try.

Everest growled deep in his throat, and pulled her

back, shaking his head. He wasn't going to let her go after Noah herself. He wouldn't risk losing Stacy, too.

"It's my fault," Stacy sobbed. Her heart was pounding out of her chest. Every second he was still down there mattered; didn't Everest understand that? But Everest only looked stubborn, holding on to her arm tightly.

Stacy looked back toward the water. *He hasn't come up at all.* Stacy shuddered, picturing Noah at the bottom of the river. *It's been too long,* she thought desperately. If Noah was still underwater, he would have died from lack of air. *Maybe he was washed ashore down the river,* she thought. But in her heart she knew too much time had passed. *Noah must have drowned.*

Another minute went by and Tucker, Wink, and Page had gathered around Stacy and Everest. Tucker began to howl the saddest howl Stacy had ever heard. She fell to the ground and buried her head in Page's fur, sobbing. Suddenly, Everest barked sharply. Stacy looked up. Noah was wading out of the water, his tail wagging. He was drenched, but not choking, not even breathing hard. Shaking water from his coat, Noah headed toward Stacy, the necklace hanging from his mouth.

"Noah!" she gasped, as if the wind had been knocked out of her. Noah trotted toward her, looking incredibly pleased with himself. Stacy ran to Noah and threw her arms around his neck. "You're *okay*," she said, and pressed her face against his soaking-wet fur, hugging him tightly.

Stacy hugged Noah for a long time. When she finally sat back to look at him, she asked, "Where did you find it? Was it down at the bottom?"

Noah nodded. Stacy stared at him. It seemed crazy, but . . .

"Were you just wandering around underwater looking for it?" Noah shrugged, then nodded again, looking sheepish.

Stacy swallowed hard. It was impossible, wasn't it? But then, Basil was incredibly, unnaturally fast. No animal could run as fast as Basil could. Did Noah have special abilities, too? "Noah," she asked quietly, "can you breathe underwater?"

Noah let his tongue loll out, his face smug, and nodded again. Stacy felt her eyes widen. "Wow," she said. "*Wow.*"

Two of the wolves in her pack, she suddenly thought, had special powers. *How did this happen?*

She had always known the wolves in her pack were special. But, Stacy now realized, maybe she had never known exactly *how* special.

SEVENTEEN

STACY WANTED TO spend more time thinking about Basil's and Noah's powers and what they might mean. But right now, they had a rescued animal with them, and they needed to help her.

"How is she, Tucker?" she asked quietly. The small dog's eyes were slightly glazed, and she was disturbingly skinny, bones sharply defined beneath her fur. Tucker nosed at the dog, who raised her head and yapped softly.

She didn't seem to have any serious injuries, but she looked hungry and exhausted. Stacy knelt and stroked her head, petting her floppy ears, and the dog gave a weak wag of her tail.

"We should get her back to the mine and give her something to eat," Stacy said. Tucker nodded. What the little dog needed most right now was food and shelter.

Food. Stacy knew there was nothing at the mine except a few pieces of fruit. She had been worried about food before, but now it was much more urgent—the exhausted dog would need plenty of food if she was going to recover.

Stacy stood up and looked around. In the distance, she could see the red-rock mesa where the mine was. She hoped the rest of the pack would be waiting there for them—she'd told them to head back to the mine if anything happened. Bending down, she picked up the dog and gently cradled her in her arms. "Don't worry," she told her. "We'll take care of you." The little dog looked up at her trustingly and then snuggled deeper into Stacy's arms.

Everest nudged Stacy, pressing his side against her legs, then looked at her expectantly. Cradling the dog carefully, she climbed onto Everest's back and took hold of his thick fur with one hand, holding on to the dog with the other. Heading for the mesa, Everest began to run at a steady pace that Stacy knew he could keep up for hours. Tucker and Noah followed.

The gentle rocking motion of Everest's run made

Stacy feel sleepy. She ached all over. Through blurry eyes, she saw shapes in the distance, near the train tracks that had brought them into the desert. A small gathering of buildings—a town, maybe?—and a scattering of tents and cabins, clearly a campground of some sort. Maybe that was where the little dog had come from.

She would take her there when she was better, Stacy decided, tucking the little dog more closely to her. She already hated the idea of giving her up, but the dog might have a family that loved her. Stacy owed it to her to try to find them.

Before that, though, Stacy and her pack would help the dog get strong again.

As they began to climb the mesa toward their mine, an excited yelping came from above. Page, Wink, and Addison were making their way down the mountainside toward them, tails wagging and eyes wide with relief.

"We're okay!" Stacy said, hugging first Addison, and then Wink, as Page enthusiastically licked her face. It was clear how worried they had all been about her and the others—they must have seen them being washed away in the flash flood.

Page finished greeting the other wolves and then walked back to Stacy, curiously eyeing the small dog in her arms. Stacy looked to Basil. "I need your help," she told the yellow-eyed wolf. "I have to get to town as quickly as possible."

Basil nodded, and then followed Stacy as she carried the long-eared dog into the mine. Pulling her pajama shirt out of her satchel, Stacy made a soft nest for the little dog on the floor of the cave and tucked the hem of the shirt around her. "I'll be back soon," she said softly. "And I'll bring you something to eat." The dog blinked up at her with big sleepy brown eyes.

Stacy turned to Tucker. "You'll take care of her?" Tucker nodded, his face serious and determined, and lay down, curling his body protectively around the little dog. Satisfied that the dog would be safe, Stacy picked up her satchel and looked at Basil. "Ready?"

Once they had climbed down the mesa and were on fairly flat ground, Basil moved so fast that the scenery around them was only a blur. After a few minutes, Stacy was so dizzy that she had to shut her eyes. "Stop far enough outside the town so that no one sees you," she told Basil, gripping her thick fur.

After what seemed like an insanely short amount of time, Basil slowed to a trot and then stopped. Opening her eyes, Stacy looked around. They were in the shelter of a patch of scrubby sagebrush. She could see the few adobe buildings that made up the town not far away, including—*Yes!*—a small market.

Hopping off Basil's back, Stacy ran her fingers through her hair, trying to work out the worst of the tangles. She had dried off on their run, but she suspected she still looked bedraggled. Humans cared about that kind of thing, and she didn't want anyone getting curious about her.

"Wait here," she told Basil. "I'll be right back." Basil wagged her tail encouragingly as Stacy set out for the market.

The door to the store whooshed open without Stacy touching it, and she stopped in the entranceway and gazed at the aisles of food.

This was a tiny town and campground. This *couldn't* be the biggest food store in the world. But she had never seen so much food in one place. There was bright packaging with pictures of cookies and crackers, piles of fruits and vegetables, loaves of bread in plastic wrappers. Stacy took a tentative step forward, holding on to her satchel. She had the fifty-two dollars she'd brought. How much did food *cost*?

"Well, hi, there," a voice said, and Stacy whipped around. She hadn't noticed the old man behind the cash register.

"Hi," she said awkwardly.

"Camping with your folks?" the man asked. "You look like you've been out for a hike."

"Oh." Stacy put up a hand and touched her hair self-consciously. "Yes. Camping."

The man turned back to his newspaper, and Stacy picked up one of the plastic baskets near the door. *These must be to put your food in while you're shopping, right?* The man didn't seem to think she was doing anything strange, so she took the basket and began to look around the store.

There was a jar of peanut butter on one of the shelves and Stacy's stomach growled. She'd loved peanut butter the few times she'd managed to get her hands on a jar back in the taiga. The label on the shelf said *peanut butter $2.99*, which Stacy thought must be how much it cost. She took one jar and backtracked to grab a loaf of bread in its plastic bag as well. Much to her surprise, the bread was already sliced, so she wouldn't need to use her knife.

The most important thing, she reminded herself, was to feed the hungry little dog. The dog would need protein to build her strength back up. Stacy didn't like eating animals, but at least the meat here was already dead.

There were refrigerators of meat all down one side

of the store. Stacy browsed, reading the labels. Beef . . . pork . . . Stacy didn't like the idea of eating a fellow mammal.

Turkey dogs! There were packs and packs of them. Campers back in the taiga cooked hot dogs all the time, and Page and the wolves always sniffed the air, their mouths watering. Stacy picked up a package. It said they were already cooked and safe to eat, even without cooking them further. Stacy loaded her basket with the hot dogs. They would make a great treat for the wolves and Page, as well as the little dog.

Heading back to the cash register, something caught Stacy's eye. There, on one of the shelves, was a sign that said *S'more Station!* Beside it were boxes and bags of graham crackers, marshmallows, and chocolate bars. Stacy couldn't believe her luck. She'd wanted to try s'mores ever since she first heard of them.

Looking into her basket, she did some quick math. She could afford to buy them, but it would use up just about all her emergency money.

She couldn't resist. *Who knows when I'll get this chance again?*

Up at the cash register, the old man raised his eyebrows as he rang up package after package of hot dogs.

"Having a cookout?" he asked. "Don't you need some buns for these?"

"Oh, uh . . . no, thank you," Stacy said. He was still looking at her a little strangely and she added, "We like them without buns."

After he handed her the bags of groceries, she hesitated. "You don't know if anyone's lost a dog, do you?" she asked. "A little beagle with long ears?"

The man shook his head. "I'd hear about something like that," he said. "Sometimes people will abandon their dogs by the side of the road, though."

Stacy gasped. *Who would dump a dog like they were garbage?*

"Did you find a dog?" the man asked. "If the owner doesn't turn up, you should take it to the animal shelter. Don't just set it loose."

"I wouldn't do that!" Stacy said indignantly. "If we can't find her owner, my family would love to keep her."

We certainly would, Stacy thought, saying good-bye to the old man and heading for the door. The little dog was so lovable, Stacy almost hoped that they *wouldn't* find her family.

That night, the little dog curled in Stacy's lap, her stomach bulging with food. Page lay on the ground beside them, grinning a wide doggy grin. Wink was flat on his back beside her, his paws in the air again. Everest and Addison had gone out to patrol after eating a few hot dogs, and Tucker was crunching a graham cracker while keeping an eye on the little dog. Noah and Basil were watching the fire, looking sleepy.

Stacy turned her stick over the fire, toasting her marshmallow to a rich golden brown. Her mouth was sticky and full of chocolate, and it was the best thing she had ever tasted.

The next morning, Stacy took a walk with Page and the little beagle to the campground she'd spotted the day before. The turkey dogs and rest had done wonders for the little dog. She had recovered quickly, and now her coat was shiny and her eyes bright.

I feel silly still calling her "little dog," Stacy thought. *But giving her a name would make it even harder to let her go.*

"Is this where you came from?" Stacy asked, looking down at the little dog. The dog panted up at her, wagging her tail. Stacy walked a few steps closer to the tents and RVs. *This is the only place she could have come from. If her family is anywhere, it's here.*

The little dog cocked her head to one side, watching

Stacy. "Come on," Stacy said. She led the way around the campsite, crossing between tents. A family was cooking over a camping stove, and Stacy asked them, "Do you know whose dog this is?"

The mother shook her head. "We've been here for two weeks and I haven't seen her before."

Farther on, Stacy bent down to talk to the dog. "Go on," she said. "Find your family." The little dog just looked up at her, then licked Stacy's face.

Wiping off the dog spit, Stacy had to smile. "You don't have a family here, do you?" The little dog panted, and then licked Stacy's face again, as if to say, *Yes, I do, silly*. You're *my family*.

Stacy scooped her up and hugged her. "You're part of our pack now, aren't you?" she said. "I guess you're going to need a new name." She looked into the dog's deep brown eyes, at the spots around her nose, and then to her long, feathery ears, which almost resembled pigtails on either side of her head. Stacy was reminded of a character from a book series she'd read called American Girl. Suddenly, a name came to her. *Molly*.

EIGHTEEN

THE SUN WAS setting as Stacy, Wink, and Addison lumbered slowly up the side of the mesa. Page and Molly were on either side of Stacy, keeping up with the wolves' long gait.

"Good work today, guys!" Stacy said. Addison flicked her ears, looking pleased. They'd spent the afternoon foraging for food in the desert. A couple of weeks before, the graceful wolf had come back from patrol carrying a book about edible desert plants. Stacy hoped Addison hadn't stolen it from the campground, but knew that she probably had. The fact that she had picked up such a useful book confirmed Stacy's suspicion that Addison had learned to read.

If Noah can breathe underwater and Basil can run so fast that I can only see a blur, Stacy thought, *it's not that hard to believe that Addi can read.*

Stacy patted her satchel, feeling how full it was. They had found plenty to eat.

"We'll roast the cholla buds tonight," she told the others, "and tomorrow maybe we'll grind up some more mesquite pods for flour." She and Addison had experimented and managed to bake thin, flat loaves of bread using the mesquite flour, which had a sweet, nutty taste.

Pulling a red chuparosa flower out of the top of the satchel, Stacy nibbled on it. It tasted like cucumber. She closed her eyes and listened to the peaceful winds of the desert. She really loved it here in the mesa. Her olive skin was now a dark tan thanks to days spent exploring the mesa with no shade. And she never tired of seeing the jackrabbits, quail, hummingbirds, eagles, lizards, and roadrunners that called the mesa home.

Stacy shivered and unwrapped the flannel shirt tied around her waist, gracefully slipping her arms into it as she continued walking. Now that evening had come, the heat of the afternoon was turning cold. It hadn't been this cold at night when they'd first come to the desert. Stacy stopped walking.

It hadn't been this cold . . .

She looked back out across the desert. How long had they been here? It had been weeks . . . maybe a couple of months? Winter had come.

Wink nudged at her hand, and she looked down to see both wolves gazing up at her curiously. Page gave a sharp bark.

"Sorry," Stacy said. "I've just realized. There must be snow in the taiga by now." She grinned at them. "Your fur won't be seen so easily. We can go *home*."

Stacy and the others made their way back to their camp where they informed the rest of the pack that they could go home now. They spent the night packing up their supplies and enjoying one last night under the desert sky.

"Okay," Stacy said, crouching behind a cluster of rocks near the train tracks. "The only train on the schedule today that's going the right way is a passenger train."

Everest's ears twitched, and he gave Stacy a stern look, shaking his head. Stacy knew he didn't like the fact that she had sneaked into the train station near the mesa village to check the schedule.

"I have a plan," Stacy told him. She looked up at where the flat top of the rock formation loomed overhead, at just about the height of the top of a train car. "We're going to climb these rocks and wait. When the train is slowing down before it gets to the station, we'll get onto the roof of the train. We can ride all the way to the taiga like that." Wink yapped in excitement and Page yipped along with him, her oversized ears perked up.

Noah wagged his tail, looking hopeful, but Everest was still staring at Stacy, a concerned look in his eyes. Stacy glanced into her satchel to make sure Milo was curled sleepily inside. The bat opened one eye to look at her, and she gently patted his back for a second. Looking around, she saw Molly sniffing the ground near the base of the rock formation. Suddenly a train whistle blew in the distance.

Refastening her satchel, Stacy got to her feet. "This is it!" she said. "Come on, everybody." Basil led the way, scrambling up the side of the rock. Tucker, Noah, Addison, and Wink all followed, Page balancing on Wink's back. Everest hung back a little, still looking wary.

Finally, he nodded and gave Stacy a quick lick on the cheek. He took hold of the bow that was slung around Stacy's shoulders and began to scramble up the rocks with it. *He trusts me,* Stacy realized proudly. *He knows my plans usually work out.*

The whistle blew again. The train was in sight now, chugging quickly closer. Stacy looked around for Molly.

Molly was nowhere in sight.

"Molly!" Stacy called. The dog had been *right* next to her.

The front of the train was level with her now. A sharp bark came from the top of the rocks.

"Get on the train!" Stacy called back. "I'll catch up! Molly!"

Molly yapped from the other side of the rocks. Stacy ran around and saw her rolling happily in the red sand.

"Molly! Come on!" Stacy scooped the dog up in her arms. The train was passing the rock formation. It was too late for them to climb on.

As she ran back around the rocks, the train was pulling away from them. Everest and Tucker were crouched on the roof of the very last car, staring back at Stacy and Molly with wide-eyed panic. Everest's muscles bunched as he prepared to leap.

"No!" Stacy shouted, waving him off. "I'll catch up at the station!" It didn't matter if humans saw her and Molly. They weren't wolves.

She ran after the train, her satchel banging against

her side. She caught up only a few seconds after the train pulled into the station and stopped.

Uh-oh, Stacy thought as she climbed the steps to the station platform. *How am I going to get up on the train roof?* The station was simply a platform with a small shelter at one end where the schedule was displayed. There was no way to climb up to the top of the train. And it was too late to purchase a ticket. *And I'd spent the rest of my money on s'mores.*

Stacy frowned, staring at the train. The door was open, no one blocking it. *Could I?*

She walked slowly to the train door and peered inside. There was a little entryway, a door on each side leading to rows of seats. Some of the seats had people sitting in them, but no one looked up.

There was a scratching noise above her. Stacy stepped back out of the train and looked up. Basil was peering over the side of the train. Stacy looked quickly around. No one was watching. "It's okay, Basil," she whispered. "I'll find a way up once the train is moving again."

Basil nodded and pulled her head back out of sight.

Holding her head high, Stacy stepped onto the train. She cuddled Molly closer to her and turned right, walking slowly down the aisle between the seats.

"All aboard!" a voice called, and a few moments later

she heard the train doors close. Slowly at first, the train began to move.

Stacy eyed an empty pair of seats in the front of the car. She moved toward them. If she and Molly sat very quietly, maybe no one would notice them. A voice came from behind her.

"Ticket, please, young lady."

Stacy turned around fast, hugging Molly tightly to her. Molly gave a short, breathless woof and Stacy loosened her grip. A conductor in a blue uniform smiled at her, his hand out.

"Um," Stacy said, "I don't have a ticket." Her stomach turned over.

The man frowned and looked around the car. "Do your parents have it?"

Stacy swallowed hard. "My parents aren't here," she admitted. The conductor was starting to look concerned, so she added, "I'm going to meet my family. I'm going home." *At least that part was true.*

"Do you have the money for a ticket?" the conductor asked.

Stacy felt herself turning red. She didn't know how much train tickets cost, but she was sure it was more than the few dollars she had left. "I only have four dollars and fifty-two cents," she admitted, staring down at the floor. "But I have to get to my home."

The conductor looked at her. He had friendly eyes, Stacy thought. Molly panted happily up at him and wagged her tail.

Finally, the conductor seemed to make up his mind. "Four dollars isn't quite enough for a ticket," he said. "But follow me."

Stacy followed him down the train aisle, her heart pounding hard. Was he going to kick her and Molly off the train? What did they do if you couldn't pay your fare?

They walked through several train cars and finally the conductor paused at a door that said *First-Class Dining Car*. "This way," he said, and pushed it open.

Instead of rows of seats, this car had little tables by each window. Some of the tables had people sitting at them, eating delicious-looking food. Music was playing from speakers near the ceiling.

"Sit down here," the conductor told her. He turned to one of the waitresses. "Would you get my young friend and her dog an afternoon tea? My treat."

Stacy couldn't believe it. She tried to thank him, but he waved her words away. "Just make sure you don't miss your stop," he advised. "Keep an eye out the window. We want to get you home."

With a final smile, he disappeared into the next car. Stacy sank back into her chair, amazed. A few minutes later, the waitress brought her a pot of hibiscus tea and a fancy tray with three tiers: one level held tiny sandwiches, the next little cookies and cakes, and the tippy-top contained several delicious-looking fruit tartlets. Molly perked up her ears, her tail wagging wildly.

Stacy gave Molly one of the tiny sandwiches, which looked like it had egg salad in it. Molly gulped it down and opened her mouth for more. Stacy sampled one of the little chocolate cookies—Molly couldn't have chocolate, after all, it was toxic to dogs. It melted deliciously in Stacy's mouth.

She felt a little pang of guilt at the thought of the wolves and Page sitting on the hard metal top of the train while she and Molly rode in luxury. She tucked several tiny tuna sandwiches into her pockets to give to them later.

"All right, Molly," she said, rolling up her sleeves. "We've got work to do."

NINETEEN

STACY SLOWLY CHEWED the last little dessert, a tiny lemon meringue pie, savoring its deliciousness. Molly, who had happily eaten her way through half the food, was curled up asleep in Stacy's lap. Overhead, Stacy could hear an occasional pawstep on the roof above her, too quiet for anyone who wasn't expecting it to notice. Peeking in at Milo again, Stacy saw that the bat was also fast asleep. She had offered him a crumb of pastry, but he hadn't been interested.

Stacy, full of food, felt sleepy, too. Leaning back in her chair, she looked out the window at the scenery going by. The orange-red of the desert biome, with its flat-topped mesa and tall, thin hoodoos, had changed to snowy white, with pine trees dark against the snow.

Blinking, Stacy realized that the snowy forest outside looked familiar. They weren't far from the taiga.

"Wake up, Molly," she said, picking the dog up. "We have to get off the train soon." Molly grunted and cuddled sleepily into Stacy's arms. Grabbing her satchel, Stacy hurried out of the dining car and through another car full of passengers.

The door to the passenger car slid shut behind her as she entered the space between cars. There was a metal door in the side of the train that led out. Stacy examined it, trying to figure out how to open the door.

I have to get out, she thought, anxiously aware of how quickly they were speeding through the forest. The metal door looked heavy, and there was a rotary wheel. *Maybe that held a latch closed?* Stacy narrowed her eyes, trying to figure it out.

Restlessly, Molly wiggled in her arms and yapped to get down.

"Shh!" Stacy said, glancing nervously at the door back into the passenger car. She needed no one to notice them. If people saw a kid fiddling with the train doors, they would try to stop her. "Stay," she said, putting Molly down.

If I turn the wheel . . . It was heavy and stiff. Stacy had to use both hands, throwing all her weight against it. At first, it seemed impossible to move. Gritting her teeth, she took a firmer grip and tried again.

Slowly, the wheel began to turn and the heavy latch unlocked. Stacy grabbed hold of the big handle and yanked the door open, sliding it back.

Cold air gusted through the opening, and Stacy shivered. It was so much colder here than in the desert! And the train was moving so fast. *Can I jump and not get hurt?* Stacy hesitated.

Then she stuck out her chin. She *had* to do it. She just had to do it in a smart way.

Looking outside, she knew where they were. "Everest!" she called, hoping that the noise of the train would muffle her voice from the other passengers. A gruff bark came from above. The wolves could hear her.

"The train's going to slow down in a few minutes to take that big curve before it goes into the taiga," she called, remembering the layout of the tracks. "We should be able to jump when it slows."

There was a pause, then another bark. Her pack was ready.

Picking up Molly, Stacy took a deep breath and steeled herself. The train was beginning to slow. *Wait for it . . . wait for it . . . NOW!*

The train slowed to take the curve, and Stacy leapt.

There was a moment when it felt like she was flying. Then she hit the ground hard and fell, banging her knees as she rolled. The snow was cold and soaked through her jeans immediately. Automatically, she shielded Molly and Milo from the ground. Stacy heard several thumps and a yelp: the wolves and Page had jumped, too.

Stacy stood up, brushing snow off herself as well as she could, and looked around.

Everest was climbing to his feet, looking ecstatic to be back in the forest. Tucker and Basil were rolling in the snow, while Wink and Page chased each other in excited circles. Molly wiggled out of Stacy's arms and jumped into a snowdrift, then jumped back, looking repulsed by the cold. Stacy reached down and picked up some snow, formed it into a snowball, then threw it. Noah raced after it, his tail held high with excitement.

Something nudged her leg, and Stacy looked down to see Addison looking up at her. Addison jerked her head, indicating something not too far away.

A sign, Stacy realized, following Addison's gaze. A big carved wooden sign, positioned so that it could be seen easily from the railroad tracks. Stacy walked closer, Addison by her side. The other wolves, along with Page and Molly, followed them curiously.

When they got close enough, Stacy read the sign aloud. "'Entering Great Taiga National Forest.'"

There was a moment of stunned silence from the rest of the pack as Addison communicated with them about the sign and what it meant, and then the wolves began to yelp in joyful excitement.

Stacy felt a little dazed, but warmth began to spread through her, despite her snow-soaked clothes. "The developers can't build the golf and ski resort here," she said. "We did it. *We did it!*"

Dropping to her knees, she hugged Wink. "It was the pictures we sent," she said. "Because we proved an Arctic wolf pack lives in the forest, the government is going to preserve it. And it all started when you accidentally got your picture in the paper."

Wink barked softly and licked her face, and then all the wolves crowded around Stacy while Page and Molly both tried to climb into her lap. *We did it,* Stacy thought. *We saved our home.*

It was a long trek through the taiga to their cave. By the time they made it, Stacy's feet were numb and her clothes were stiff with ice. The wolves' fur was full of ice, too, and Molly kept shaking her head to free her long ears from the snow.

Pulling back the branches and boulders, she entered the cave and looked around. It was just as they'd left it. Stacy's books were lined up on her homemade bookshelf, and she ran her fingers across them, delighted to see all her old favorites. The firewood Stacy had left piled at one side of the cave was still there, undisturbed, and Basil hurried over to it and picked up a log in her mouth, eager to build a fire. Stacy watched as Basil placed it in the stone hearth. Suddenly, a small flame appeared, as if Basil had sparked a fire with her nose. Stacy blinked her eyes. *That's impossible.* She chalked it up to her exhaustion. Noah wandered toward the waterfall at the back of the cave, no doubt to make sure the water was still there. Tucker and Everest stretched out near the cave entrance, keeping an eye on the world outside. Addison headed for the table, eyeing the newspaper they'd left there so many weeks ago. And Wink and Page were exploring the cave with Molly, looking happy to introduce the newest member of their family to their home.

Opening her satchel, Stacy gently lifted Milo out. He took up his usual spot near the bookshelf where Fluff was roosting, the pile of seeds Stacy had left for her nearly gone.

Stacy looked around the cave. Everything was the way it should be, minus the abundance of chicken poop, which Tucker was already tidying up. As the cave began to warm from Basil's fire, Stacy collapsed happily into her rocking chair. *It's good to be home.*

TWENTY

"**JINGLE BELLS, JINGLE** bells," Stacy sang, draping a garland of dried apple slices across the Christmas tree. Those were the only words she knew to the song, a faded memory she had from before the helicopter crash.

Outside, more snow was falling. Molly had claimed the best spot in the cave, directly in front of the fire. It turned out she was a little bit of a diva in that regard. Addison was next to Molly, keeping an eye on a baking pumpkin pie. Stacy sniffed appreciatively at its sweet smell. The other wolves were out playing in the snow—Stacy could hear Wink yelping happily as he and Noah wrestled in a snowdrift. Page was burrowing in the snow with Droplet and Splat, while Basil ran circles around Everest. And Tucker was helping Stacy decorate the cave for the holiday.

It looks good, she thought, standing back to take a critical look around. As well as the garlands of dried apples and pinecones hanging on the big Christmas spruce tree the wolves had dragged into the cave, there were silvery angels and snowflakes Stacy had crafted from birch bark. There was an evergreen wreath hanging on the other side of the cave, and presents piled under the tree, wrapped in newspaper. There was something for everyone, right down to a little perch Stacy had carved for Milo, so that he'd have somewhere comfortable to hang near the fire when he visited them.

Addison barked softly, and Stacy looked over to see that the pumpkin pie was almost done. The big pot of beet and apple soup by the fire smelled delicious, and the roasted salmon with pumpkin seeds looked almost ready to eat, too.

"Okay, I'll let them know," Stacy told Addison. She hung one last birch snowflake on the tree and headed out the cave entrance.

Outside, Noah and Wink had finished wrestling and were now playing tag with Page, Droplet, and Splat, who dodged between the trees, their tongues lolling out

as if they were laughing. The young timber wolves had thrived hunting for themselves while Stacy and her pack were gone, and now looked almost full-grown.

Everest and Basil were pushing giant balls of snow with their muzzles. As Stacy watched, Basil and Everest lifted one on top of another and then Tucker placed a pumpkin on the top. *They're building a snowman,* Stacy realized. *They're definitely not normal wolves.* The thought struck her once again: *Why* was her pack so different from other wolves? *How* did they come to have unique powers? Basil had her super speed. Tucker, the ability to heal. Wink could fall long distances and not get hurt. Noah could breathe underwater and Addison could read. And Everest . . . Stacy had always joked that it was like Everest could read her mind. But now she wondered if that might actually be true. *How did they get these abilities?*

Almost on cue, Everest looked up at her questioningly, and Stacy smiled at him. "Dinner will be ready in a few minutes," she said. He barked in acknowledgment and ran to inform the others.

Stacy turned back toward the cave and stopped, surprised.

There was a large box sitting in the snow outside the cave. She bent and carefully picked it up. It was wrapped in pretty paper with a pattern of Christmas ornaments on it, and a red bow. The tag on it said *Stacy*.

Stacy froze, her heart beginning to pound harder. *It couldn't have been here long,* she thought, *or the snow would have covered it.* Who knew she lived here? No one. No one who could *write*, anyway, or who had wrapping paper. Her wolves had abilities, yes. But this present could not have been wrapped by paws.

Slowly, Stacy unwrapped the box, her cold fingers fumbling with the paper. Inside the box was a layer of pristine white tissue. Stacy reached beyond the tissue and pulled out a beautiful winter coat. It was a rich green color with lots of pockets and a fake fur trim around the hood . . . it was perfect. A small card fell to the ground. Stacy picked it up and read it. *Happy Holidays, Stacy,* it said. *I hope you have a very happy New Year. Love, Miriam.*

Miriam. Stacy gulped. Miriam had stood up to help preserve the taiga from development. She loved animals and the wild. She knew where Stacy lived—somehow— but she hadn't come with a bunch of humans to try to take her from her pack. She had left her a *present*.

Stacy took a deep breath, trying to calm down her pounding heart, telling herself it would be all right. She trusted Miriam, she realized. Miriam might know

Stacy's secret, but Stacy was sure Miriam would never betray the pack.

Stacy wondered if she'd ever see Miriam again. She had a lot to learn about humans still, but getting to know people like Miriam was worth the effort. Maybe someday Stacy would spend more time in the human world. But for now, her place was in the taiga.

A bark came from behind her, and Stacy turned to see Everest herding Droplet, Splat, and Wink toward the cave entrance, Page and Noah trailing along behind. Basil was carefully putting two twigs in the snowman for arms, while Tucker held it steady.

There was a lot more to learn about her wolf pack, Stacy realized. Maybe even more than she needed to learn about humans. Where had they come from? Why were they so special? How did they acquire the unique powers they had, and were there other wolves with different abilities somewhere in the world?

Someday I'll find out, she decided. *But for now, I'm happy just to be part of this wild pack, to be home, and able to rescue animals. This is where I belong.*

STACY'S FAVORITE WORDS
FROM THE BOOK

bedraggled—out of sorts or messy in appearance. Example: *Stacy ran her fingers through her hair, trying to work out the worst of the tangles. She had dried off on their run, but she suspected she still looked bedraggled.*

bolster—boost or support. Example: *Stacy was happy she'd been able to bolster Basil's spirits, if only for a moment.*

cacophony—a loud combination of sounds. Example: *An entire cacophony of coyote howls could be heard, first coming from the north.*

cladode—a flat part of a plant's stem that resembles a leaf. Example: *Stacy took her hunting knife and began chopping the purple fruit off the top of the cactus cladodes.*

dubiously—to be filled with doubt or hesitation about

something. Example: *Stacy looked at the mineshaft dubiously.*

grueling—extremely physically demanding. Example: *After several grueling months of treatment, Molly survived and moved with Stacy and Page to Los Angeles, CA.*

hoodoo—a tall weathered rock formation. Example: *Farther south was a cluster of tall, spindly rock formations Stacy knew were called hoodoos.*

inquisitively—expressing curiosity. Example: *Addison was peering up at Stacy inquisitively.*

legible—text that is clear enough to read. Example: *There was what looked like an abandoned church on one end of the row of buildings, and a blacksmith on the other, its sign weather-beaten but still legible.*

maneuvered—moving carefully, possibly around obstacles. Example: *Taking the stick in one hand, she maneuvered it through the mesh at the top of the cage.*

monotonous—a sound that doesn't change tones and

is considered boring. Example: *Even though the subjects were fascinating to Stacy, the villagers all had rather monotonous voices.*

perimeter—a boundary or contained area, either invisible or with a fence. Example: *"Basil, set up a perimeter!" Stacy said in an urgent, hushed voice.*

podzol—dirt that has become soft and acidic from evergreen tree needles that fall on it. Example: *Wink and Noah ran off in front of Stacy and began digging in the soft podzol.*

proficient—very skilled in a particular task. Example: *Stacy suspected Addison knew how to read. That knowledge made the graceful wolf particularly proficient in things like baking, where exact measurements were required.*

prototype—the first model or completed version of a product. Example: *Stacy showed the wolves the first prototype of her Wolf Pack Hip Pack.*

reverently—quietly and respectfully. Example: *"Wow,"*

Stacy said reverently, crouching to the cave floor and running her fingers along the bow.

rouse—to wake someone from sleep or a trance. Example: *Wink attempted in vain to rouse him with his nose while Tucker checked Noah for more darts.*

sauntered—to walk in a slow and casual way. Example: *Wink sauntered up to Stacy and innocently dropped a mouthful of crumpled peonies in her lap.*

slunk—the past version of "slink," which means to move quietly and stealthily. Example: *Everest and Wink slunk through the long grass over to where Stacy and Page were standing.*

stifle—to hold something in, like an emotion. Example: *Basil seemed to stifle a laugh.*

striated—striped. Example: *The two sides of the canyon were striated with different layers of red, yellow, and tan rock.*

sullen—gloomy or sad. Example: *Stacy got out of her chair and walked over to a sullen-looking Basil.*

transpired—took place. Example: *"Okay," Stacy began, taking the camera from Tucker and trying to put the pieces of what had just transpired together.*

vantage point—a place to get a good view. Example: *Jack began to scramble up a rock pile to where he had a decent vantage point over part of the taiga.*

THE REAL-LIFE MESA BIOME!

The biome Stacy and her pack travel to in *Wild Rescuers: Escape to the Mesa* is inspired by several United States national and state parks located in southern Utah, including Bryce Canyon National Park, Zion National Park, and Snow Canyon State Park.

In fact, Stacy loves the desert so much, she recently purchased a home for her mother there where she and her pets frequently visit.

Stacy has also featured the Minecraft mesa biome in many of the series on her YouTube channel: www.YouTube.com/StacyPlays. Her series *Mystic Mesa*, *Mesa Valley*, and *The Candy Mesa* all include the awesome backdrop of this majestic biome. She is currently planning several episodes of her *Minecraft Field Trip* series to the mesa biome as well.

The author hiking in Snow Canyon State Park.

MEET THE REAL-LIFE MOLLY!

Stacy adopted Molly from a rescue group in Washington, DC, in 2011. Her name was originally Diva, but Stacy didn't think it suited her because Molly was very sick with heartworm when she was rescued. After several grueling months of treatment, Molly survived and moved with Stacy and Page to Los Angeles, CA, to an apartment under the Hollywood sign. Guess she was a diva after all!

Yes, that's the same dog! Molly before and after Stacy rescued her.

Breed: unknown, although she looks like a beagle/Cavalier King Charles spaniel mix

Age: unknown (approximately 8 years old)

Rescue date: August 12, 2011

Favorite activity: sleeping

Favorite foods: bananas, apples, edamame

Fun fact: Stacy named Molly after the American Girl Molly McIntire because her ears resemble pigtails!

Name:
Coyote Peterson

Current job / past job:
Host of the Brave Wilderness network's animal
adventure shows on YouTube, including *Breaking*

Trail, Beyond the Tide, On Location, Dragon Tails, and *Coyote's Backyard.*

How did you get the name Coyote?
It's a nickname I have had since I was around eight years old. My mom gave it to me, and it originates from me chasing roadrunners around in the deserts of the Southwest in the hopes that they would lead me to lizards that I could then catch before the roadrunner ate them. My mom called me Coyote because like the famous Warner Bros. cartoon . . . the Coyote was always chasing the Road Runner!

Have you traveled to a desert biome? What animals did you see?

I have been to deserts in both the United States as well as Australia. Both locations were filled with elusive animals, including lizards, snakes, insects, arachnids, birds, and small nocturnal mammals. Finding animals in the desert is all about exploring at the right time of day or night when the temperatures are cooler.

A lot of people are afraid of mammals like coyotes, mountain lions, and wolves. Having been up close with them, what would you say to people who are afraid?

Large mammals, especially predatory ones can be intimidating. It's always best to admire these animals from a distance. NEVER run from a predator. That ignites their motivation to hunt and attack. Animals don't want to interact with humans, and most encounters happen by chance. These are not animals to be afraid of, but you must have a solid respect for their predatory nature.

What should you do if you encounter a mountain lion when you're hiking?

Make yourself look big and scary, loud noises will often scare them off. If one does attack you and you are not able to fight it, curl into a ball and protect your neck and face. Attacks from mountain lions are very rare and often happen as a case of mistaken identity.

What should you do if you come across an injured wild animal?

It's always best to quickly alert your local wildlife rehabilitation center. These professionals will help you address the situation or will come to your and the animal's aid. Never try to handle or interact with an injured wild animal as they are likely in pain and very scared. This can result in them biting or attacking you and causing injury to you or further injuring themselves. Calling for help from animal experts is always the right thing to do!

Do you consult with local wildlife experts on your adventures?

Yes. On almost every shoot we have experts who we work with. Getting the proper permissions for locations and permits to interact with animals is a very important aspect of the preproduction work we do.

What advice do you have for people who want to do what you do?

Anyone can start a YouTube channel, but it takes commitment to keep it going. When it comes to animals, the best place to start is school! Studying animals, their habitats, and their history is a great way to learn about the life around you. If you pursue a career working with animals, a great place to start is volunteering at wildlife rehabilitation centers. These centers are often nonprofits that can use all the help they can get when it comes to taking care of their animal residents. Get involved, be willing and ready to get your hands dirty, and certainly always express an excited love for animals and the work you aspire to do!

About Coyote:

Coyote Peterson travels the world with his team to document the animals that call our planet home. His YouTube channel, Brave Wilderness, boasts over 12 million subscribers and more than 2 billion views. He also loves to write, and you can find his books *Brave Adventures: Wild Animals in a Wild World* and *The King of Sting* online and in bookstores everywhere.

ACKNOWLEDGMENTS

Thank you to my amazing, smart, beautiful, and loyal Wild Rescuers readers and YouTube viewers. Every time I meet some of you at conventions and bookstores, I am completely blown away by how awesome each and every one of you are. You are the reason I get to play games, make videos, and write books every day, and I'm so thankful for your support.

Thank you, Mom, for taking me to Zion and Bryce Canyon National Park (where I first fell in love with the mesa biome), and for being the best brainstorm buddy, creative confidant, and petsitter anyone could ask for.

And thank you, Dad, for taking me camping in Shenandoah National Park, and for helping me so much with my business while I was writing this book.

To my Nan and Papa for giving me such wonderful memories of helping them around their farm. I can't grow a potato or make jam in real life, but I'm an expert at it in Minecraft.

Thank you to all my friends, fellow Minecrafters,

aunts, uncles, nieces, nephews, and cousins who have shown up to my tour stops and cheered me on. I love you all.

Thank you to my editor, Sara Sargent. These books were written during two very tumultuous years in my life, and her understanding and grace helped me through some very tough months.

I feel like I don't have the adequate words to properly thank Vivienne To for another book filled with the best illustrations any author could ask for. Getting to work with you has been a highlight of my career. Thank you again for taking such care with my characters, and turning my crazy ideas into reality.

Thank you, Jessie Gang. You are simply divine, and your positive energy is all over this book. I'm so grateful.

And thank you to Camille Kellogg, Meaghan Finnerty, Caitlin Garing, Paul Crichton, and all the other wonderful people at HarperCollins Children's Books who I've worked with.

And to the amazing people who have been part of team StacyPlays this past year: Madeline Lansbury, Nathan Onandia, Tyler Focus, Madison Finlinson, Jacob Finlinson, Andy Rosenberg, Louis Mensinger, and Meg Campbell—I don't deserve any of you. Thank you for all your help.

And, of course, I have to mention my little pack—Page, Molly, Polly, Milquetoast, and Pip. Page is very sick as I am writing this from my cabin to send the book to the printer, and I don't know if she will be here when this book is published, but she will always be with me.

Page and Molly love you; go rescue a dog!

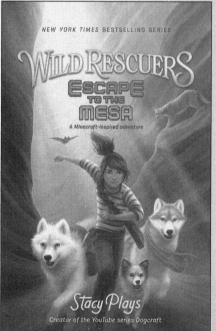